MYTH

THE ORIGIN OF MAN

by Aaron Steiner

Strategic Book Publishing and Rights Co.

Strategic Book Publishing and Rights Co.
12620 FM 1960, Suite A4-507
Houston, TX 77065
www.sbpra.com

ISBN 978-1-61204-865-9

In loving memory of Bruce Lee and Jimi Hendrix

PROLOGUE

In the twilight of the pale red landscape, set next to a small body of water, a large golden bell-shaped rocket ship was being prepared for launch by a reptilian crew. Dressed in form-fitted, dark grey spacesuits a shade darker than the brownish grey color of their scaled skin, members of the small crew attended to their assigned duties at various points throughout the large ship, their senses heightened as they focused on the pre-launch protocols.

Made up of the Anunaki's elite, fifty crewmembers were serving on this important mission. Inside the ship, the rest of the crew lay dormant in the amber glow of the ship's stasis chamber. One by one, engines and thrusters slowly came to life as systems were calibrated and brought online, creating a low hum that grew increasingly louder. The ground crew briefly glanced at one another in a knowing symbiosis as they completed each of their individual systems checks.

The ship had located the ancient landing site from the air by the large pyramids that had been built there long ago, and they set their spacecraft down on its lakeside terrace to refill the reserves of H_2O that fueled their ship. Commander Ea and his pilot, Anzu, were the first to put on their protective suits and helmets and step out onto the firm ground. They were now off exploring the Martian wilderness and taking samples while the necessary crewmembers had been awakened from their stasis automatically to refill and do maintenance on the ship.

A long hose that extended from the bottom of the craft sucked lake water into the ship's holding tanks. In the meantime, Ea and Anzu were working with tester kits out in the strange environment and found that the water was drinkable, but the atmosphere was not breathable. They recorded all their findings on one of their ship's computer's Mae Stone crystals and added a brief explanation as to why the detour had been necessary.

"Kaarrrtuuuk!" announced the lower deck commander. "Lord Ea is on board!" As one, the assembled crew paused in their work and tipped their heads, crossing their right arms briefly over their chests in salute. They uttered faint hissing sounds, a sign of respect and unity, as their proud reptilian prince and commander, Lord Ea, and his second-in-command, Lord Anzu, entered the room and removed their space helmets. A series of horns tapered sleekly back along the ridges above Lord Ea's large eyes and over the top of his dark green, scale-covered head. The commanders wore dark green hooded cloaks with a sun insignia on the left lapel over their grey spacesuits, and their thick tails moved about the floor casually behind them as they strode proudly across the main aisle. The two reptilian commanders towered over many of the lower ranking crewmembers. Deck commander Enursag approached Ea and knelt down on one knee.

"Lord Ea, the H_2O reserves are full; the ship is at the ready and awaits your command."

Ea placed his right hand on his deck commander's shoulder, signaling that he could rise. As Enursag rose to his feet, Ea turned and began to remove his protective suit. Well built in stature, standing over ten feet tall, the long and short horns along the ridges of his skull tapered down his back and tail and up and over his shoulders; his rough, dark green scaled skin fading into a tan underbelly. As Anzu removed his suit, it could be seen that he was physically similar to Ea in many ways, but he was more greenish-grey and tan with differently shaped horn patterns along his head.

Leaving the lower levels of the ship, the two went up to the control helm located in the upper portion of the vessel. Under the craft's dim interior lighting, the dark gray metallic material that composed the walls glittered at times as they walked down its hallways, almost alive in a strange way. The ship had been built with a self-maintaining, organic-hybrid technology that gave it a highly functional, ergonomic aesthetic.

Ea and Anzu arrived at the ship's bridge where domed, holographic crystal view screens adorned an array of computer consoles, set with illuminated multicolor crystalline control components. Ea walked over and stepped up onto the central command platform where a large chair arrayed with colorful crystal control panels awaited him. He sat down and Anzu went to his command station to begin systems checks.

"Open the main view screen," Ea commanded.

As the iris in the main screen of the ships control room slowly opened, the bridge was filled with the reddish-orange light of Mars. When the lizard men's large, wide eyes adjusted to the light, the nearby pyramids of the ancient Martian landing site could be seen, brightly lit by the pale red planet's setting sun.

In a dim, soft amber light, most of the ship's crew lay dormant in the liquid stasis tanks that lined the walls of the lower deck like honeycombs. From his station, Anzu monitored the ship and checked on the crew to be sure everything was in order for the rest of their journey. "The crew is in stasis and the reserve tanks are synchronized, my lord."

Lord Ea nodded his satisfaction with the report and gave the command for the launch sequence.

The countdown began. When the thrusters were engaged, the commanders could instantly feel the surge in power, the vibrations being intense, while outside the craft a small cloud of red dust began to swirl. The computer's onscreen monitor showed the countdown symbols and their ship lifted off. Up, higher and higher through the clouds of Mars it went, pushing its way through the upper stratosphere. Within moments, the craft was engulfed in black, star-filled space. Ea and Anzu silently contemplated the small spot of light within the center of their main screen that was Earth in the distance and then set the ship's controls to automatic and retired to their stasis chambers for the rest of the journey.

This crew's mission was to reach a planet of abundance, rich in resources...especially gold, for gold would ultimately be the salvation of their home world. The planet was called Earth. Once there, these beings would establish a command center, harvest its gold and eventually create the human race. They come from the trinary star system of Sirius, seven stars away. From the planet Rizq, in orbit of the sun Sirius B...they are Elohim...the Anunaki— they were the Gods.

Chapter One

E a awakened slowly as dormant consoles began to activate, giving off a soft amber glow within his darkened stasis chamber. He was floating in one of the stasis tanks that honeycombed the walls of the ship's lower interior. Filled with a gold-flecked liquid, they were designed to protect the crew from the harsh detriment of the radiation in space. A soft beeping indicated the activation of the ship's internal controls that were set to turn on when they reached Earth. Like the rest of the crew, command entered the stasis tanks once star charts had been checked and the flight plan programmed. Telemetry of the approaching planet was now coming online, as the chamber filled with a soft, bluish glow while their ultimate destination was being calibrated by the ship's computer. He slowly reached for the controls on the upper left side of his tank and punched the release hatch. Instantly, its liquid was released, as the low thrumming of the tank came to a stop. The hexagon-shaped lid of the tank slowly lifted and the stasis rack extended outward.

Ea's chamber had been pre-programmed to awaken him a few moments before the others. Sitting up, he looked around the dim room. The honeycomb of stasis tanks were beginning to come alive with beeping lights as his crew began to awaken. Climbing off the rack, he put on his cloak. Once he was sure that his deck commander and his pilot appeared to be waking without a problem, he proceeded to the upper level, back to his command.

When he reached the bridge's command deck, on the main monitor, against the starry blackness, Ea could see that they had indeed reached their destination. There, in all its white capped swirly blue eminence, was the planet Earth. Absently, he marveled at how small of a planet it actually was in comparison to his own, yet when it came to natural resources, it held so very much.

"And that's why we're here..." he whispered to himself.

Lord Ea was soon joined on the bridge by his flight commander Anzu, who was a closely related cousin and highly experienced in the art of aviation. Acknowledging his pilot, he sat down in his chair upon the command platform to focus on the planet's approach. Anzu took his place at the helm and switched the automatic pilot back to manual so that he would be in control of the ship.

As they entered the outer atmosphere of Earth, an orange glow began to rise from the bottom of the view screen.

"Lord Ea, my readings are showing that we are entering the planet's atmosphere too fast. We must slow our approach or it will tear us apart. I recommend that we first make two passes around the planet's moon." Anzu said.

Ea was anxious to get to the surface, but not at the risk of destroying the very ship they were arriving on. "Yes, Anzu," he said, "Do whatever you think is necessary to insure our safe landing."

After making two rotations around the small Earth satellite, their ship's speed was reduced enough to enter Earth's thermosphere safely. They could now clearly see the large land masses separated by deep blue waters through the hazy clouds below. They curiously observed the snow-covered poles and the dark blue hue of the oceans as well as the greens and browns of the large landmasses. After making two passes around the surface of the planet, the ship was getting closer to solid ground. They were searching for the homing beacon of the Earth's original discoverer, the ex-king Alalu, when finally they zeroed in on a transmission coming from some marshlands located at the mouth of a river along a coastal shore of one of the large land masses. The area would one day become known as Iraq, or Ur—at the mouth of the Euphrates River, in the Persian Gulf.

"Lord Ea," Anzu said, "this craft is much too heavy to land in the marshes, and the Earth's gravity is too strong for us to touch down on dry land!"

"Then land us in the ocean!" Ea shouted anxiously.

Anzu made one more pass around the planet and carefully set the ship down into the ocean waters along the coastal shore, near the marshlands from which the signal they were tracking was coming. When they splashed down, Anzu immediately filled the large craft with oxygen to keep it afloat.

The crew was now fully awakened from their stasis as the honeycomb of tanks that lined the walls of the ship's lower levels were in their final stages of activation. In unison, the chamber doors opened, releasing the occupants within. On the ship's intercom speaker, all throughout the ship, Alalu could be heard.

"My brothers...you've made it!—Welcome to Earth!"

Anzu followed the signal and drove the great ship toward it like a boat. The transmission led them to where the wide ocean waters narrowed into a channel with land on each side of them. They ultimately found themselves entering a shallow marshland.

Ea spoke into the ship's intercom, "All crew members...put on your suits and grab some strong cables. You must get out of the ship to pull it through the shallow marshes!"

The crew exited the craft through a hatch on top of the ship, attached the ropes and slowly pulled the large vessel through the marsh water. Alalu's signal was getting stronger.

"Pull faster!" Ea shouted to the crew impatiently from the bulkhead doorway.

Then, from behind the tall grasses, the spacecraft that Alalu had stolen from Rizq could be seen reflecting the light of the sun near the bank of a wide river that went inland. At the sight of the gleaming ship in the distance, the pace of the crew members in the water quickened. His heart beating quickly in his chest, Ea put on his protective suit. He could not wait any longer, and he jumped into the marsh waters, swimming with bold strokes toward the shoreline.

As he swam toward the shore, Ea could see the green meadows behind Alalu who was there waving his arms to signal them. When he could feel firm ground under his feet, he stood up.

As he got out of the water, Alalu came running toward him. He greeted Ea with a powerful embrace and said to him, "Ea my boy...Welcome to this strange new planet!"

It was a powerful moment when Alalu and Ea continued their embrace in proud silence. Alalu was his father-in-law and Ea bowed his head respectfully when they were done.

The crew was now approaching the shore with their massive spacecraft.

"Anchor the ship in the water to avoid the mud that lies ahead!" Anzu shouted to them.

The crew did as they were instructed and then waded ashore to bow before their ex-king Alalu as he welcomed them to Earth. The last to depart the great ship was Anzu. After he jumped into the water and came ashore, Alalu welcomed him with locked arms and a warm embrace, for they were closely related. After Alalu had welcomed all who had arrived, Ea got up on top of a large rock to address the group.

"My brothers... our vanquished king informs us that this world contains the gold we will need to heal the breach in our world's atmosphere." The crew was excited to hear this as they looked at one another with a mutually assured sense of confidence. "This world also contains a vast range of other natural resources, all within an oxygen-rich, breathable atmosphere. I propose the new outpost we build here be named—Eridu . . . Home in the Far Away."

"On Earth, I am commander, so I expect your efforts to be optimum and diligent. I do not need to remind you that this is a life or death mission…the very fate of Rizq is in our hands. Failure is not an option."

As Lord Ea left his platform, the crew tipped their heads and hissed softly. They would not let their prince down. More importantly, they feared the repercussions of the missions failure even more.

As they began to set up the camp, Ea discussed their first order of business.

"We will need to start building walls out of earth to protect our encampment," he ordered the crew. With that underway, he went back into their ship and had a message beamed to Sirius to inform the council that they had arrived on Earth successfully.

Shortly thereafter, the sky's colors began to change to a pink, reddish hue when the sun began to set and then disappear behind the horizon. The crew had never experienced such a thing, and they worried that a great calamity was upon them.

Alalu laughed at their apprehension. "There's nothing to fear, brave crew. It is just the setting of the sun. The day is done on this planet. You must get your rest, for the nights here are very short."

Just as they were getting comfortable, the darkness of night was upon them, and then the storm came. Lightning flashed all around them, followed by loud thunder and rain. The winds were strong and the crew hunkered down within the ship. No one slept that night.

At dawn, there was much rejoicing and backslapping when the sun finally returned. In the new day's early morning light, Ea now assessed the rest of what must be done to fully establish their Earth base encampment.

✦ ✦ ✦

Over the next six days, the team constructed its mission control center on the banks of the mighty river near where it met the gulf. Upon first sight of this new world, the crew was mystified by the abundant alien plant life that seemed to extend as far as the eye could see. The new planet was quite similar to their own, with its lush vegetation and terrain, yet it was wild and uncultivated. Here, the multitude of plant life within the jungles filled the sky with high-arching canopies that thatched together above their heads. The tall, greenish-barked trees of the vast botanical forests seemed to literally scrape the sky.

Ea assigned teams to perform specific tasks, as they proceeded to build their encampment. He chose crewmember Engur to work on the water purification—they would need clean healthy water to drink and they did not yet know the effects of the microbes to be found in the Earth water. He then assigned crewmember Enbilulu the task of creating an artificial lake in the marshlands to catch fresh rainwater.

The next day, when everyone was busy with their assigned tasks, Ea and Alalu walked to a sun lit area among the grass and trees where all sorts of herbs and fruits grew. Having developed a keen interest in the growing of food, Ea was constantly asking his personal vizier Isimud about the different forms of vegetation that they encountered. Isimud showed him a large, round honey fruit that he had plucked from a tree and broke it open. He shared a piece with Ea who took a large bite of the succulent fruit.

To his surprise, he enjoyed it very much, so Ea had Isimud and crewmember Guru go around and gather all the edible foods they could find.

The team now had clean water and food, but they were not satisfied in what they would require. On the fourth day, they brought tools ashore from the ship and crewmember Kulla was to be in charge of making bricks, laying foundations and fashioning more permanent dwellings.

On the fifth day, Ea called upon crewmember Ningirsig.

"I would like you to fashion a boat made of reeds so that we can accurately measure the surrounding marshlands," he told him.

Ea called on crewmember Ulmash to determine which birds

were good for food, and he then summoned crewman Enbilulu to speak with him about another very important project.

Ea took him to where the river waters began to drain into the gulf.

"This is where I will need you to create a ditch and a dam to separate the carp from the other fish that are suitable for food," he explained.

Enbilulu did as was asked, then took it one step further and created a device that would ensnare birds that were suitable for food as well. Ea was impressed.

On the sixth day of their stay, Ea took some time to consider the legitimate dangers of the local wildlife. He summoned commander Enursag, whom he had assigned to document all that crept and walked within the local jungles, and spoke with him.

"My lord," he began, "I've found many intriguing species of wild animal in the surrounding areas and am actually quite astounded at their ferocity." He proceeded to describe some of the creatures to Ea, who became most concerned with his findings.

Upon fully assessing the true nature of the local wildlife, he assigned a team to build a large fence around the compound, making it clear to them that it was quite imperative that they finish it before nightfall.

The teams cut down trees to build the fortified fence, while others finished the pod like structures within the encampment as they installed their thatched, reed roofs.

Anzu brought laser rifles from the ship for extra protection, as well as some transmission equipment that he set up in Ea's quarters. By night, all was complete and the crew gathered inside the encampment for the evening. When they had settled in and looked back on their week, Ea, Alalu and Anzu were quite pleased with all they had accomplished.

On the seventh day, Ea and his teams rested. There was a meeting, and upon a unanimous decision, it was decided that they would indeed name their encampment Eridu—Home in the Far Away. Ea stood and the crew came to attention as they prepared for his announcement.

"I, Ea, your lord and commander, vow to keep my promise that Alalu be named commander of Eridu." There were a few low murmurings because of the conflict regarding legal ascension, but he expected that and chose to ignore it. The majority of the crew uttered words of encouragement.

Alalu then rose, ready to speak. Ea stepped to the side. "I, Alalu, your acting commander on this world, accept this title. I praise you, Lord Ea, for your skillful design and craftsmanship of Eridu and more importantly, for the depth of your wisdom." The crew cheered and Ea bowed his head as he accepted their praise.

For many nights, Ea watched the moon's changing cycles and recorded them onto a Mae Stone crystal. He had ultimately decided to call these lunar cycles' *months*. He also recorded Earth's passage around the sun with all of its seasons onto a Mae Stone crystal. In time, he decided to call the phenomenon of Earth's passage around its sun a *year*, marking the beginning of each new year at the point when Earth came closest to his home world's sun, Sirius B.

While on his daily walking inspections outside of Eridu, Lord Ea came to find that he did not care for the tangled vines and wide leaves that cluttered the trails they had made, so he assigned mechanized trimming vehicles to clear wide paths. This enabled their teams to go back and forth easily between the many flower pod-like outbuildings that they had constructed throughout the surrounding jungle.

✦ ✦ ✦

While the Anunaki were a cold, efficient race, at times Ea's thoughts did sometimes wander to reminiscence of his family back home, and how he had ultimately come to this strange planet.

Ea was the firstborn son to Lord Anu, the king, conceived by a

concubine. His brother, Enlil, was the second born son to Lord
Anu by the Princess Anatu, a royal…making him the "legal heir"
to the Riziqian throne. Their young sister, Ninmah, had also been
born to a concubine. Her name represented the fact that she was
the firstborn daughter to Lord Anu. As were the Rizqian females,
she was a very beautiful, birdlike creature, full of wisdom and
always a quick learner.

Their father had decreed that Ea espouse Ninmah so that their
firstborn son would become the legal heir to the throne, but
Ninmah had become enamored with Enlil. The dashing young
commander was statuesque and handsome, with light brown scales
and a series of long and short horns along his cranium ridges that
tapered back behind his head, around his shoulders and down the
center of his back and thick tail. She had allowed herself to become
seduced by Enlil's charms, and eventually she discretely bore him
a son whom they named Ninutra.

Lord Anu had been angered when he found out about the affair
and he punished Ninmah, declaring that she would be forbidden
to have a spouse…ever. Anu abandoned his decree of espousal and
Ea ended up marrying a princess named Damkina—Lord Alalu's
daughter. They now had a royal heir, a son named Marduk, his
name meaning—One in a Pure Place Born.

As for his brother Enlil, he had his son, Ninutra, but not by legal
marriage…and he never did become married.

He wondered when, or if, he would see any of them again and
whether they would ever get to see this strange, new world.

That all depended on the success of their mining operations. So
far, they had extracted many varieties of metal from the local gulf
waters—iron, copper, but very little gold. They needed it to protect
their dying world's atmosphere…they needed gold. As well as being
a base element of their technology, more importantly, the gold
would be turned into a colloidal. The fine dust would then be
dispersed into the breach in their home world's upper atmosphere
to stop the catastrophic loss of its oxygen and internal planetary

heat, that would soon leave their world devastated. The disaster was initially caused by their ex-king Alalu's irresponsible decisions to use nuclear blasting within their planet to heal problems that had been developing within its core. That is why his father had come to challenge and overthrow him in a fair match of grappling. It was then that, under the cover of darkness, Alalu had left the planet for fear of his life in a stolen spacecraft and come to Earth.

The Elohim—leaders on Rizq, were amazed that Alalu wasn't dead when they had received the transmission from him, coming from a distant planet. He had told them that he found a way to save their world and heal the rupture in its atmosphere, but they must give heed to his conditions. There were those who felt that it was most likely a deception and that he was probably hiding in some remote, concealed place.

After the council had consulted their commanders and savants, it was discovered that the transmissions were indeed coming from beyond an asteroid belt within the Seventh Solar System.

The king informed the assembled council to send an acknowledgement to Alalu, and from their tower at the Place of Celestial Chariots the transmission was sent.

"Alalu, this is Anu. We are pleased to learn of your well-being, and there was certainly no reason to leave Rizq. To be perfectly honest…I feel no hostility towards you. But Alalu, if you have indeed found gold upon your departure, this is wonderful news! Our world may very well be saved…!"

The words quickly reached Alalu and he soon responded. "I will share my findings, but first, you must tell the princes to gather an assembly to declare *my* ancestry supreme. Have the commanders make me their leader and let the council pronounce me king, to replace Anu on the throne."

Bold words indeed…when Alalu's message reached Rizq, they were both shocked and dismayed. How could Anu be dethroned? What if Alalu *was* lying and attempting to pull off some kind of clever deception? Where exactly was this place that he had found and was there actually gold there?

Sages, the wise and the learned had been summoned for council.

The turn of events had created quite a commotion within the assembly when, finally, the eldest among them spoke out.

"I was once Alalu's master. At one time, I taught him of the Celestial Mechanism. I told him of the watery planet Earth and of its golden veins. If Alalu has journeyed into the asteroid belt of the seventh star—Sol—planet Earth is where he would have gone."

Among the assembled princes, it had been his brother, Enlil who was the first to speak out.

"It is Lord Alalu who is responsible for the enormous natural catastrophe that now threatens our world. His right to our throne was immediately compromised when Lord Anu wrestled him in a challenge of grappling...and he lost."

"If there is indeed gold on Earth—actual proof will be needed! And if it is there...is there enough to protect our atmosphere? I would also like to know how he even made it through the systems asteroid belt." The rest of the council agreed with him. Many questions needed to be answered, as well as some actual proof.

The words of the assembly were transmitted to Alalu and he agreed to send his findings to the council on Rizq and explain the process of how he survived the perils of his journey.

Alalu went and retrieved the crystal shard from the sampling machine that had been recording his findings and inserted it into a transmitter within his ship, sending its data back to the home world. With Alalu's findings transmitted...he demanded that the council declare him king.

The sages were aghast at the idea, especially concerned by the thought that he would one day cause more havoc on their world if he were to ever have access to their atomic weapons again. They felt that he *must* have used powerful weapons such as these to blast through the asteroid belt and that the celestial repercussions could eventually prove to cause even more unknown calamities and disasters. The whole assembly was in a state of horrified uncertainty. The altering of the kingship was indeed a grave matter. It was then that Ea had spoken up and told of how his marriage to Alalu's daughter, Damkina, was to bring about the union of the two clans. Ultimately, this is why he had volunteered to come to Earth as an emissary for Lord Anu and the council to determine the validity of Alalu's claims.

He had explained to the council how he would devise a way to blast through the asteroid belt with water...not fire. If there was indeed gold in Earth's waters as Alalu's findings indicated, he would find it and send it back. He also suggested to them, that if this is *truly* the salvation of the planet, allow a second wrestling and the winner shall be proclaimed king.

The princes, the counselors, the sages and the commanders, all found Ea's words to be filled with wisdom, relieved that they had finally found a solution to their dilemma. The decision was sent to Alalu and he accepted the council's terms indifferently. Alalu then transmitted his coordinates to them from the distant planet.

When Lord Anu declared it official before the council of the assembly, it hadn't surprised him when Enlil stood up to object to what he thought was a recklessly bold decision. The king's word is always final and unalterable; he should know that by now.

Ea reflected upon his time at the Place of Celestial Chariots—Nippar—his home world's space ship facility where he had consulted the sages and commanders to discuss the perils of the mission. They had discussed in depth the best ways to extract and bring back the Earth gold. From Alalu's transmissions, Ea compiled the star charts and trajectories needed, as well as Earth's geological information and encoded them into Mae Stone crystals. If water was going to be the power source for their spacecraft, he needed to know where they were going to replenish its reserves. Other important concerns had been, where on the ship would they store the water, and what would be the most efficient way to convert it to power?

It had taken them a year—or *Shar*, to plan and a Shar to prepare and by the time they were ready, the Rizqians had equipped the largest interstellar vessel in their fleet with all of the required components needed for the mission. Within their final stages of preparation, when all was in order, they named the great ship Nibiru—the Relentless Crosser of the Seas of Space.

Ea had sought out the best of the best for this mission and recruited fifty of Rizq's finest officers to be his crewmembers, and when they were ready, Lord Anu gave the operation his final approval. The mission's Mae Stone crystals were placed in their trays and the culmination of their calculated telemetries were downloaded into the ship's computer.

When the time chosen by the stargazers had finally come, the multitudes gathered at the Place of Celestial Chariots to bid farewell to the crew and their commander. Carrying their spacesuits and helmets, his crew boarded the large golden spacecraft one by one. He had been the last to board the ship. Standing on its entranceway platform, he bade the crowd farewell and then knelt before his father to receive his blessing.

Ea remembered the words Anu had said to him as if he had just spoken them. "My firstborn son: you are about to embark on a long journey and we are all in danger. May your success alleviate and remove the danger that is upon us. Go in safety, and in safety return."

His mother, Ninul, then embraced him and she spoke softly, "My son, why have you been endowed with such a restless heart? Go ...and return. Traverse your hazardous roads safely."

Ea's heart softened even further as he reflected upon his parting moment with his wife Damkina, tenderly kissing and hugging her in an intimate moment of complete silence.

Finally, he turned and locked arms with his brother, Enlil. "Be blessed and be successful!" had been his parting words.

With a heavy heart, he entered the ship and gave his cousin Anzu the command to begin the countdown for lift off. With all the crew in stasis, Nibiru was launched and Anzu headed the great ship toward this distant Seventh Sun. During the trip, they were awakened periodically to check on their course and navigate through the many hazardous and potentially dangerous environments that they came across on their long journey.

He and Anzu had both been awakened from their stasis as they approached the solar system of Sol, and when they saw the planet Pluto in their monitors, they knew they were on course. After systems had been checked, they returned to stasis briefly and were reawakened when their ship began to approach Neptune. He recalled the conversation of how Anzu had been deceptively drawn to its watery blue essence.

"My lord," he had said, "I think we should explore this planet for a useable water source."

"No, Anzu!" he replied forcefully. "What looks like water on that world, I believe is in actuality *hydrochloric acid*. This is a planet of no return. We need to keep going!" He did not elaborate and Anzu did not question the decision as he steered past the blue-green planet. They returned to their stasis chambers and were awakened again at the approach of the next heavenly body: Uranus.

Anzu had informed him that the scans of Uranus' moons were indicating there was indeed water to be found if they needed to stop, but he wouldn't risk it, so he told him to continue on toward Saturn.

When they were awakened from stasis at Saturn's approach, he remembered looking out the ship and admiring its rings in awe and with careful discernment.

Soon the pull of Saturn could be felt upon their spacecraft, and with a skillful quickness, Anzu maneuvered their ship through the dangerous debris field that could have easily crushed them. It was after the dangers of Saturn's rings had passed, that the two retired to stasis. They were awakened once again to the soft sounds of alarms when it was time to navigate past Jupiter.

The pull of the large planet had been tremendous and almost

overpowering. It brought the Rizqian craft in very close to its outer stratosphere, but Anzu was able to skillfully maneuver past it. The lightning that was generated by the spacecraft's passage was quite spectacular as it crackled intensely all about their ship. Slowly, they moved past the enormous planet, and the two commanders were able to breathe easily as they went back into stasis until the next hazard awoke them.

When he and Anzu had been awakened by a warning of asteroids, Ea knew they had reached the asteroid belt, one of the most hazardous elements of their long journey. He quickly prepared and activated the special water cannons that he designed and had installed into the ship. They aimed the machines at the oncoming asteroids and blasted them with powerful streams of water. The onslaught of boulders created from the destruction of an ancient planet known as Tiamat was incessant and almost overwhelming at times. But the cannons had worked well and a path was cleared. Ea kept the machines spinning at full force and ultimately they passed unharmed through the thick layer of the asteroid belt that they had been forced to pass through. He remembered how relieved they were to finally see the sun again.

Amidst their elation, another alarm had sounded. It was to alert them that the water consumed to create a pathway was excessive and that what was remaining was not enough to create the fuel needed for the rest of their trip. Within their monitors, in the deep darkness of space, they could see Mars reflecting the sun's rays.

"Anzu, there is where we will find water, on the planet Mars. You must land the ship there," he told him.

"Yes my lord," he responded, and with skillful precision, Anzu steered their ship toward Mars. When they arrived, he made a circle around the planet to slow their descent. Its gravitational pull wasn't very strong, making their descent relatively easy for him to handle. Mars had been a magnificent experience with its snow-capped poles and reddish hue. He remembered quite distinctly how they could see the glimmer of the lakes and rivers below them as they made their descent to the planet's red, dusty surface ... It had truly been a spectacular sight to behold.

Lord Ea brought his mind back into the moment, as he realized he needed to clear thoughts of this nature from his head. He was scheduled to meet with his close companions, Lucifer and his personal vizier, Isimud soon. It was Lucifer who had been chosen to be the outpost's chief security officer and was one of Ea's favorite cousins. He and Isimud were to accompany him to a very important upcoming meeting that the home world had set up, to discuss their mission's yield out of the gulf waters.

Leaving his office, he met with the two, who had been waiting for him in the outside hallway. Lucifer was a well built and handsome individual, even by Rizqian standards ... with his fine, long horn patterns, golden-scaled skin and sleek muscular body. The shimmering golden color of his scales was considered unique and they faded to a cream at his chest and underbelly. The golden, horned ridges above his eyes tapered sleekly up and around his head, smoothly down his back and tail, and up over his shoulders. His vizier Isimud was also very physically fit and the large array of multi-horned patterning on his head reflected a strong intellect. His coloring was more of a simple olive and cream. They both wore dark hooded cloaks about their shoulders and carried a large, double bladed sword at their side.

The two walked behind Ea as he entered the dimly lit, tan stucco conference room within Mission Control of Eridu. Set prominently in the room's center was a small table with illuminated crystal shards set into it. These were the crystal Mae Stones that contained all the programmed information about their Earth mission and all of the information that ran the missons computer systems and machines.

Holographic topographies on tables and brightly lit charts and wall maps of various Earth continents filled the room. Ea's highest-ranking commanders were seated in dark spiny chairs at dark metallic tables and several of them were studying one topographical map in particular. When they saw Lord Ea enter the room, they all rose in attention and crossed their right arms against their chests as they tipped their heads in salute.

"As you were," Ea said. The officers sat down and Ea looked over at Ennugi. He was the mission's chief officer of excavations. "What information do you have for me?" he asked.

Ennugi was stout, had long thick horns, was very muscular, and his scaled skin was a blotchy pale green and tan color that faded to cream at his chest and underbelly. The horned ridges above his eyes tapered abruptly up and around his large cranium, down his back and thick tail and up over his broad shoulders.

It was one year ago that Ea had begun the extraction of gold from the local waters. They had been using their great ship to suck the water into its holding tanks and pass it over crystals that would extract the metals from it. The teams would work for six days in a row and on the seventh day, they would rest, taking an account of their week's return. There always seemed to be an abundance of copper and iron in the gulf waters, but very little gold.

"My lord, as you know...the gulf water operations are providing a minimal yield...and the process has proven to be quite time consuming." Ennugi looked up from his charts. "Although we have discovered many valuable secondary resources to gather and process, our main goal—the acquisition of Earth gold—remains elusive."

"The swamp waters of the gulf are obviously deficient," Ea said flatly. "We will just have to move the operations out into deeper ocean waters."

The decision was acknowledged unanimously, and the crew soon untied the great ship from its mooring. The craft was then taken to the deeper waters where it had originally splashed down and they recommenced their water extraction operations in the open sea. Passing the saltwater over the crystals within the ship with great care, they found that there was now definitely more gold among the metals than they had been extracting from the marshland waters.

"I will send word to Lord Anu about these new findings," Ea muttered to himself, shaking his head, "but he will have to be informed that there is still not enough gold to send back yet."

With apprehension toward the success of their new endeavor in the open waters, Ea has his personal pilot, Abgal, fly over the lands to survey for alternative resources. Inside Alalu's ship, Ea re-studied the information that had been gathered and recorded on the ship's Mae Stones about Earth, its landmasses, minerals and overall geology. He spoke with Alalu and asked him about his earlier findings, and Alalu showed him where he thought the most likely gold veins within the Earth would lie.

From aircraft, Ea did surveys with Abgal daily, their travels taking them over mountains, valleys, great rivers and oceans. Using a device that could penetrate the soil with its scans while recording all of its findings into a Mae Stone crystal, they learned many things about the Earth.

✦ ✦ ✦

Back on Rizq, Lord Anu made a demand: he wanted a ship sent back with at least *some* gold. A celestial alignment was upon them and the planets would be at their closest. He contacted Ea on Earth and before long, his son's image faded into view within the crystalline viewing monitor on his desk.

"Ea…" he said calmly.

"Yes, my lord," Ea replied from within the large crystal.

"Whether you have enough to send or not, we need gold here, regardless. There is an opportunity approaching that we do *not* want to miss. Repair Alalu's ship and fit it for a cargo transport."

Ea exhaled dramatically, "As you wish father," he said, and the communication ended.

Late that night, Ea and Abgal went to the spacecraft that Alalu had commandeered so long ago to begin determining what needed to be done to prepare it for cargo transport. Once inside the great ship, they made a shocking discovery.

"My lord," Abgal said under his breath, "I have just discovered that there are still some very dangerous nuclear missiles hidden onboard this ship."

"What?" Ea said. This was indeed disturbing news and he knew they needed to do something about it. "Abgal, we must move these weapons immediately." He thought carefully for a moment and then decided. "We will hide them in a secret cave that I know of, deep within the mountains."

They did just that, and once they were done, Ea instructed Anzu to repair the ship and retrofit it for cargo transport. Anzu was greatly skilled in rocket ship mechanics and he was able to successfully repair the enormous spacecraft. He brought thrusters back online and carefully recalibrated the ship's Mae Stone crystals. However, when he found out that the ship's weaponry had been removed, he was outraged.

"You did what?" he shouted loudly.

"There's no reason to be angry Anzu," Ea told him. "We hid them in a secret location. You must understand . . . there is nothing good to come from the unleashing of these devices, on the land *or* in the heavens."

"But Ea," Anzu said, "how will the ship be expected to travel safely through the asteroid belt without these weapons, as Alalu's ship does not have the luxury of having water cannons built into it! We should let Lord Anu decide this matter," he demanded.

The beamed transmission from Lord Anu was that, after much consideration of both their arguments, he'd had to take the matter before the council. "And they have decided," Anu said, "that they agree with Ea's decision. The old path will have to be found and utilized."

"My lords," Abgal boldly stepped forward to address both Ea and the hologram of Lord Anu contained within the crystal dome. "I would like to volunteer to fly Alalu's ship back to Rizq in Anzu's place."

Ea looked at him, "You do realize how dangerous the trip through asteroid belt will be?"

"I understand the risks, my lord, but this is the gold that will save our world. The successful completion of this important journey will insure my family's name a place in history," Abgal said as he bowed respectfully.

With Anu's consent, Ea accepted the brave proposal. Anzu was to remain on Earth, while Abgal prepared for his mission. The star gazers on Rizq calculated the appropriate date for departure and the ship was loaded with all the gold that they had managed to gather. When the time of alignment arrived, Ea gave Abgal a small tablet containing the collection of Mae Stone crystals he would need for his trip.

Sitting in his commander's chair at the helm of the large vessel, Abgal inserted the crystal shard Mae Stones he had been given into his ship's computer consol. The Mae's were specially pro-grammed with all the information the craft would need to find the path through the asteroid belt that was created when they had arrived. When he pressed the crystal panel that activated the ship's engines, the droning hum of the rockets sounded like music to him as they gave off a brilliant orange glow that could be seen by all those who had gathered to watch the launch.

The crewmembers stationed in Eridu all came to bid farewell to Abgal. From a safe distance, they watched in silent awe as his craft gave off a great roar while it rose into the sky and made its way toward outer space. News of the ship's departure was transmitted to Rizq, where they waited eagerly for the gold to be delivered safely.

Abgal confidently guided the spacecraft as he looped around the moon to slingshot himself and gain speed. He then guided the golden ship toward Mars. When he finally got there, he used the same maneuver once again and headed toward the asteroid belt, where he eagerly anticipated the challenges it posed. The Mae

Stones were glowing, as Abgal used them to find the small pathway through the perilous field of floating debris. Fate seemed to be with him and he ultimately managed to locate and safely traverse the narrow corridor within the large asteroid belt.

The transmissions from Sirius were now coming in strongly, as Abgal checked his coordinates before putting himself into stasis, only to be awakened periodically to do routine system checks.

Ultimately, Abgal was brought out of stasis when his ship started getting close to the Siriun home world of Rizq. When he got to the ship's main deck, his home world's sun of Sirius B could now be seen within the ship's main monitor, revealing itself as a reddish glow in the darkness. Abgal was relieved that the long journey was almost over. For him, it was a *truly* magnificent sight to behold.

The ship's computers had the home planet locked in, but Abgal switched the controls to manual when he entered its upper atmosphere. He could now see the breach in their stratosphere quite clearly as he made three loops around the planet to slow his descent. As his ship approached the capitol city, he could see its gleaming spires, geometrically woven roadways and well-manicured, lush green overgrowth. Landing the craft at the Place of Celestial Chariots, he was joyously greeted by a multitude of the populace.

When he opened the hatch and got out of the ship Lord Anu approached the victorious cosmonaut and locked arms with him.

"Greetings, Abgal!" Anu said warmly.

The containers of gold that he had brought were unloaded from the cargo bays and presented before the crowd. It was a most dazzling sight to behold. Abgal raised his arms and he shouted to the assembled masses.

"Salvation is here!"

The crowd gave a great roar and Abgal was given a royal escort to the palace to rest and tell the tale of his perilous journey, and of his time spent on the strange and distant world.

The gold was taken to their top scientists who began refining it into a fine dust. After many experiments and much testing, the gold dust was now ready to be transported via rocket ship to the upper atmosphere. There, it would be dispersed and held in place from the ground by electromagnetic beams that were governed by a series of Mae Stone computer crystals.

Their application worked, and the giant hole actually began to heal itself.

In the palace, there was much rejoicing and prosperity was expected to return to the planet. Lord Anu sent word to Earth that the gold was working and that they needed to diligently continue their extraction efforts.

Much to everyone's dismay, when Rizq passed closest to their sun, the gold particles were disturbed and dispersed. This caused the healing in their atmosphere to disperse as well and the hole went back to being as big as it once was.

Disappointed with this course of events, Lord Anu decides to send Abgal back to Earth with more crew members. As they prepare the ship, the king appoints his royal pilot Nungal to assist with navigating the long journey.

✦ ✦ ✦

When Abgal and Nungal returned to Earth with a fresh crew, there was much joy in Eridu with many greetings and locking of arms. Their reunion was bittersweet however, considering the recent failure caused by the Siriun sun.

Over the years to follow, Ea worked diligently to optimize the water extraction's yield. However, when the time came to send Nungal back one celestial passage of Rizq later—a Shar—the yield of gold was minimal at best. Ea knew that his home world would be disappointed yet again.

He traveled over all the landmasses of the Earth, still doing continuous surveys for an alternative solution. When he spoke with Alalu on how to reconsider their gold options, the vanquished king suggested a completely new approach. His idea was to obtain the gold from where it originates...from *within* the planet. In the southern region of a heart-shaped land mass, across the ocean, he pointed out an area where the dry land came together and its innards spilled forth. Ea took a liking to the idea, and he named the area—the Abzu—Birthplace of Gold.

Ea was now in a meeting with his commanders in the Mission Control room of Eridu. They were examining the various holographic readouts of the Abzu area that had been gathered within the Mae Stones.

"My lord, we have been studying the extensive Earth surveys from your data and from the Maes taken from Lord Alalu's ship," Ennugi said, as he gestured toward one of the floating holograms in a large domed crystal monitor, "and we have been examining your suggestion for the region in which to expand our mining efforts."

Ea gently stroked his chin whiskers as he stared at the image. He knew that the extensive amounts of information that had been gathered would one day prove to be invaluable. Ennugi pointed to a specific area of the holographic topography.

"Based on the scans you took, we believe that this area of the land mass that you have suggested will most certainly provide us with the gold that we are seeking." Ennugi was speaking of what is now the southern section of the continent of Africa—the Abzu.

Ea thought about it briefly as they all waited attentively. His preliminary studies of the scans of that region and the ones contained within Alalu's Mae Stones had definitely shown high-level readings that indicated gold ore in great abundance, deep within the bowels of the planet.

"This plan sounds quite promising...considering that our gulf water extraction efforts have been fruitless and ineffective," he said with disdain. "I will transmit our findings to Lord Anu and request an expansion of our operations into the Abzu."

Ea contacted the council to inform them that the planet Earth was *indeed* rich with gold; it just needed to be extracted from deep within its veins, not from its waters. He told them there was gold that they could attain in great abundance existing in a region a continent away, in a place he called the Abzu.

In the palace on Rizq, they were astonished at the news. After ending the communication with Earth, savants and councilors considered Ea's words deeply. They were all in agreement that the gold must be obtained, and there was much discussion on how to obtain it from deep within the planet. Enlil however, was not as easily convinced.

"Council, I object to this course of events. Do I need to remind you how we were assured before that the gold we needed was ready and available from the Earth waters? We waited and waited. Now, we are being told something entirely different. It is now to be obtained from *within* the Earth? The monumental task we are speaking of undertaking is beyond imagination. Proof is needed and a plan that ensures success must be put into place!" Many agreed with Enlil.

"You have made some valid points, my son," said Anu. "Perhaps you should go to Earth to obtain this proof and create a plan for us from there." The assembly gave unanimous consent, and Enlil was soon sent to planet Earth.

Enlil made the journey to Earth with his chief lieutenant Alagar as his copilot.

When they arrived, Ea greeted his brother with a warm embrace. "It is good to see your safe arrival, my brother." He gestured toward an aircraft that was parked nearby. "I can have Alagar fly the two of us down to the land of the Abzu right away." Enlil agreed and they left.

Once they were over the Abzu, the commanders proceeded to scan and survey the land. They scanned deep into Earth and they found much gold. The biggest problem was that it was mixed with dirt and rock, unlike the gold that they had taken from the gulf waters. When they had completed their surveys, the group returned to Eridu to discuss their findings.

After the commanders had assembled, Enlil stood up and made an abrupt announcement. "Eridu will no longer do," he said to them as he looked around the room. "But I have a plan..."

This was curious to Ea, who first had to deal with the knowledge that his brother was suddenly sent there to join him; *now he wants to step in and dictate how things will be done?*

"I propose a great mission," Enlil continued. "We will send for more teams from the home world to build new settlements... We *will* obtain gold from inside the Earth, but it will have to be separated and refined. Sky ships will also have to carry the ore, so landing sites will need to be established as well."

"So, tell me brother, who will be in charge of the new settlements in the Abzu?" Ea asked him.

Having remained silent, Alalu spoke up now as well, "And who will be commanding Eridu?" he asked.

Anzu also shared their concerns. "Yes... and who will be in charge of the sky ships and their landing facilities?"

"It's not for me to say," Enlil told them cryptically. "We will petition Lord Anu to come here, and he can decide the appropriate assignment of these duties."

Anu agreed to come to Earth and he appointed Nungal to be his ship's commander.

Departing on their journey, Nungal piloted the king across space, past the planets, to the Earth. Along their way, they detoured slightly as they made a loop around Mars. The King had become quite enamored of the red planet, and he observed it closely before continuing on their way. When they had finally reached Earth, they made a loop around its moon to slow their approach. Anu observed it closely and wondered to himself if gold might possibly be found there as well. They ultimately entered Earth's atmosphere and splashed down in the ocean waters near the marshlands of

Eridu. Prior to their arrival, Ea had fashioned sailboats out of reeds for the occasion and was waiting there to give Lord Anu a royal welcome.

Because he wanted to be the first to greet them, Ea was alone in the lead boat. When small craft reached the ship, Ea was finally reunited with his father. Wearing a large red cloak and a thin, golden crown, the king's resemblance to Ea was quite apparent, except that Anu was much older and had longer horns about his head and shoulders.

Ea bowed before him. When he stood up, Lord Anu gave him a big hug and shouted, "Ea, my son!"

The reception then escorted Lord Anu to the center square of Eridu where all the Rizqian crew had assembled. They stood in perfect rows to welcome their king in a royal manner, as Lord Anu entered the courtyard—Ea walking next to him, his arm crossed over his chest. The loyal reptilians all dropped to one knee and raised their right arms in an open-handed salute as the Siriun king proceeded down the path in a slow, stately gait. Before the king's throne stood Enlil with Lord Alalu. They were attired in dark green ceremonial cloaks with golden sun insignias on their left lapels.

Lord Anu hardly acknowledged Alalu; his eyes focused on Enlil. It was quite apparent that Anu was ever so proud of his son Enlil, the legal heir to his throne. Though firstborn, Ea was not born to Anu's official spouse, yet here he stood dutifully, the first one sent to a new world on behalf of the kingdom. *Better yet,* Ea thought wryly, *I get the additional honor of watching my younger "official" brother stride in and take command.* Regardless, Ea remained poised as Lord Anu hugged Enlil with a strong, heartfelt embrace.

"My son, it is good to see you." Enlil stood back and bowed before his father. When he stood up, Anu embraced him to his chest again.

As Alalu stood there next to them, he was a little uncertain of what to do. The king looked over and finally extended him a greeting.

"Now, Alalu," Anu said cheerfully, "let's lock arms as comrades." Without hesitation, Alalu stepped forward and they warmly locked arms with one another.

An elaborately spiked, iron throne had been constructed for the king and he sat down upon it. For the evening meal, a sumptuous feast was prepared by Lord Anu's entourage for all the newly arrived, as well as the stationed crew. The crewmembers who had come to Earth prior were most appreciative of the foods from their home world. Although they found the food on this new world to be edible, it lacked much of the tastes of home.

Anu sat at the head of the table, flanked on either side by his two sons. While the royal family ate and spoke lightly of administrative matters, it was hard for them to ignore the looming issue that would have to be addressed immediately—the division of power between Ea and Enlil.

Ea decided against direct questioning of Anu simply because that was not the way things were done. He would have to wait patiently for his father to address the subject in his own time and abide by whatever decision was made. Once Lord Anu was ready to retire for the evening, the king and his party were escorted to their makeshift, temporary reed sleeping quarters for the evening.

The next day was the traditional seventh day; a day of rest, and everyone celebrated Lord Anu's arrival. It was a day of festivities, backslapping and celebration, one that truly befitted the arrival of a king.

✦ ✦ ✦

On the following morning, the commanders discussed with Lord Anu what had been done on Earth and what now needed to be done.

Anu wanted to be shown the Abzu, so they traveled there via shuttlecraft to let him see the area for himself.

Upon landing in the lush green of the proposed excavation site, Lord Anu was given a tour of the surrounding terrain. After he had made a thorough inspection of the area, he consulted his sons.

"Although this gold extraction effort will most certainly be a difficult task, we need it desperately," he told them. "No matter how deep this ore resides, it must be obtained! Our world's very survival is *depending* upon it."

"The two of you will be given the tasks of designing the equipment that will be needed and assigning the necessary work-forces. We will need a large machine to bore into the earth, and the means to separate gold from dirt and rock. Once you have built an adequate landing site, the equipment will be sent from the home world, along with more workers."

At this point, Anu was also considering how useful the creation of a processing station on Mars could be to the mission, but he kept the idea to himself for now.

Ea and Enlil bowed their heads in agreement with their father's wishes, and upon returning to Eridu after two full days in the Abzu, they held a council to assign tasks and duties.

It was late afternoon, and Ea had completed his rounds and station reports. He was next scheduled for an important meeting at central control. With his vizier Isimud by his side, Ea entered the dimly lit room to find Lord Anu, Enlil and three of his high commanders, Ennugi, Lucifer and Anzu standing over a large table of illuminated blueprint holograms. They all appeared to be in deep discussion and he was certain he knew what it was regarding. The group looked up upon noticing his arrival and he spoke out the moment they did.

"I know what is going on here," he bellowed suspiciously, "and I would like to remind you all that it was *I* who established Eridu," he pointed out. "With these expansions and the creation of addi-tional settlements, Eridu is now being referred to as an Edin—the Home of the Righteous Ones. It should rightfully be me command-ing the Edin. Enlil can be in charge of the gold extraction in the Abzu," he told them forcefully.

Enlil was angered at the very thought and told his father so.

"These claims are unfounded! I am obviously more suited to run Edin, for I am more experienced as a commander as well as in the duties needing to be performed here. Ea is quite knowledgeable of the Earth and its inner secrets. It was he who discovered the Abzu ...let him be in charge of it."

Anu listened carefully to the angry words of his two sons and he became concerned that the conflict could potentially endanger the entire mission. To Lord Anu, the royal succession was much less important than obtaining the gold. He thought that perhaps one of them would have to return to Rizq and rule in his place.

After weighing the full depth of the situation, the king made a most startling suggestion.

"My sons, the three of us could simply draw lots. We can allow the Spirit of Chance determine who will return to the throne on Rizq, who will run Edin and who shall go to the Abzu."

The brothers were silent, quite surprised by their father's bold suggestion.

"Yes...we shall draw lots and let the Fates give us a decision!" he told them.

The tasks were inscribed onto metal squares and placed in a small box. The three shook hands and then drew lots...and by lots the tasks were divided.

Anu would return to rule on Rizq.

Enlil would take command of Edin to be—Lord of the Command, as his name rightfully indicated. He would now be in charge of establishing the new settlements and of the spaceships and their crews. His domain was to be all of the lands up to the ocean.

Ea was given domain of the waters and the lands past the waters. He was to command the Abzu and apply his ingenuity into obtaining its gold.

Enlil was quite pleased with the lots results and he accepted his fate with a gracious bow to his father. But within Ea there was a great dismay, for he was not as pleased with the results and the outcome of this event did not sit well with him. Logic dictated that Enlil should succeed him because of their laws of succession, but a small part of Ea would not let him forget exactly how his own father came to power. A coup d'état, internal strife among their people, the planet's atmosphere dying…he held his tongue and accepted his fate, but he did not wish to leave Eridu and the Edin.

Anu could tell that Ea was upset, and he spoke to Enlil. "We will let Ea keep his home in Eridu. It should be insured that his being the first to splash down be forever remembered."

"Ea will be given a new title. He shall from hence forth be known as Enki—Earth's Master."

Enlil bowed to his father and acknowledged to Ea his new title. "You shall be known as Lord of Earth and I shall be known as Lord of the Command," he told him. It was a gesture of respect, but for Ea it was a small consolation for being assigned away from the new command center of Edin.

Anu was relieved to have the issue put to rest. "Very well…we will gather an assembly and announce our decision."

✦ ✦ ✦

Ea and Enlil silently followed their father down the long hallway as they returned to the palace throne room, where the majority of the crew was assembled and awaiting the announcement of their decision.

Upon the entrance of the royal retinue, Ea's high commanders and everyone in the room dropped to one knee and gave salute as Lord Anu took his throne. He was provided a golden scepter that had the bodies of two snakes intertwined up its shaft with a winged sun sphere at its tip by one of his attendants, and he held it across his lap. Ea and Enlil knelt before the throne and the audience waited expectantly. Lord Anu lifted the golden scepter and pointed it at Enlil.

"Edin is assigned to Enlil," he said with finality.

The room was silent, but Ea could just imagine the thoughts of the crew as he was being reassigned.

Anu continued his decree. "Ea will command the extraction operations in the Abzu, and he will be given a new title. For being the first to establish a settlement here, he will be known as Enki—Lord of Earth…Success for the future!" He looked at his sons proudly. "I can now return to Rizq with a quiet heart." Lord Anu then turned to the court and bid farewell to the assembled crew.

Alalu abruptly stepped forward and approached Anu. "A grave matter has been forgotten!" he shouted. "When I had shared my gold findings with the High Council, it was promised that I would be commander of Earth!"

"Nor have I forgotten my claim to the throne on Rizq. For you to share all of this with your sons only…is a grave abomination. I challenge this decision!"

There were still resentful stirrings within their society about Lord Alalu's reckless use of the nuclear weaponry within their planet that had ultimately created the tremendous hole in their atmosphere. After the colloidal gold had been successfully infused to the damaged atmosphere, most were now simply concerned with addressing the pressing issue of maintaining it. Although Lord Anu had been the direct heir to the throne, he had originally lost his place to his cousin Alalu out of chivalry back when Alalu had challenged the late King Lahma for the throne…and won. Being the closer lineage bearer, Anu later usurped Alalu's throne through a challenge of physical prowess.

Vanquished, Alalu fled their home world for his life in a nuclear-armed spacecraft that he had stolen to seek out a solution to the problems that he had been held accountable for. Upon exile, Alalu had discovered this world with its accessible, abundant gold supply but his initial bad judgment about the nuclear devices that caused the problem in the first place, could never be dismissed.

Anu was quiet at first, but finally he spoke up, with anger in his voice. "We will wrestle a second time and settle this dispute, right here…right now."

The two large lizard men removed their capes and in nakedness, they began to grapple. The Rizqian champions wrestled in a mighty struggle, but in the end, Alalu bent one knee and down to the ground he went. With his foot on Alalu's chest, Anu claimed victory in the match.

When Anu removed his foot, Alalu quickly got up, grabbed him by the legs and pulled him to the ground. The two struggled for a moment when suddenly, Alalu bit off the end of one of the largest horns on Lord Anu's head and then stabbed him in the upper thigh with it, near his groin. Anu cried out in pain and fell to the ground. Alalu then took the horn and swallowed it, knowing he had *truly* hurt the king—because to a male Rizqian, their horns are important symbols of their status and male virility.

Enki ran to the fallen Anu, as Enlil kept the laughing Alalu held captive. Anu was picked up and carefully carried to his hut while he uttered curses at Alalu under his breath.

"Lieutenant...! Justice shall be swift—kill this despicable worm!" Enlil shouted to one of his guards.

Enki shouted fiercely, "No! No! Justice is within him. The horn that he has swallowed will tear him apart from the inside when his body tries to pass it!"

Bound by the hands and feet, Alalu was taken to a reed hut and held under guard where he would await his trial.

Chapter Two

I n the king's reed hut, Lord Anu was hurting badly as Enki applied healing salves to his wound. Alalu was in his hut hurting as well from the horn that he had ingested as spittle ran down his mouth and his stomach swelled.

After day three, Anu's pains subsided but his pride was still greatly injured. Enki and Enlil were by his side in the makeshift dwelling where he was still recovering from his ghastly wound.

"My sons...I want to go home immediately!"

"Yes Father, of course," Enlil said, "but Alalu must stand before the High Council to be tried and judged first."

By the laws of Rizq, seven judges were required, the highest of their ranking among them. In the courtyard of Eridu, everyone gathered for the trial of Alalu. The traditional hexagonal seating arrangement was set up for the judges with the highest ranking seat on a raised platform in the center.

Lord Anu sat in the central seat with Enki to his forward right and Enlil to his forward left. At the hexagon's points behind Enki, Anzu and Nungal were seated. At the two points behind Enlil sat Abgal and Alagar. When Alalu was brought before them and unbound, it was Enlil who was the first to speak.

"A wrestling match was held in fairness and Alalu has forfeited his throne to Anu!" he said.

Enki turned to Alalu, "What do you have to say about Enlil's claim?" he asked.

"I agree that the match was fair, and I had forfeited to Anu," he uttered under his breath.

"After his loss in the match, Alalu performed the abominable crime of attacking the king," Enlil said. "The punishment is death."

Enki looked at Alalu, "What do you have to say about that?" he asked the ex-king. There was heavy silence in the court, for Alalu would not answer the question.

Alagar spoke up. "We all bore witness to the extent of Alalu's crime...! The judgment *must* be in accordance!"

All were silent as Alalu slowly began to speak. "I...was once king on Rizq by right of succession," he began. "Anu was once my cup bearer—but he roused the princes and challenged me for the throne. I had been king on Rizq for nine circuits."

"This kingship *rightfully* should be going to my offspring and *my* bloodline!"

"As Anu sat upon his throne, I traveled the dangerous journey to a distant planet to escape death and possibly obtain the salvation for our world. And I did...I found salvation for Rizq; I found *this* planet," he told them.

"It was promised that I would be able to return to our home world to fairly regain the throne. First Ea comes here, and *he* has a claim to the throne now, through succession. Then, Enlil comes here with his direct claim to the throne through Anu. Anu then arrives on Earth and tricks Ea with this decision to draw lots. As a consolation, *he* is now proclaimed Lord of Earth'"

"Enlil is given command of Eridu and Edin; Enki is given command of the Abzu. From my chest, my shame and anger was bursting. Then, once again vanquished as Anu put his foot on my chest...it was my aching heart that he was treading upon!"

Out of the silence, Lord Anu spoke up. "My royal lineage is pure and I gained the throne from you in a fair combat of strength of prowess. You attacked me in an act of malice after you had been given a second chance and fairly vanquished...again."

Enlil announced to the court, "The accused has admitted to his crime! Let the judgment come."

"Let the punishment be death!"

Alagar, Abgal and Nungal nodded as they agreed, and they said death as well.

"Death will already come to Alalu from the large, sharp cranium horn that he has ingested," Enki told everyone calmly.

Anzu had also hoped the council would consider a less harsh punishment. "Perhaps Alalu could be imprisoned here on Earth until the day he dies," he suggested to them.

As Lord Anu considered their words, he was engulfed in anger and pity, but when he ultimately delivered his final judgment, he was calm, serious and dignified. "Alalu's fate will be to die in exile," he declared. The judges looked at each other in confusion as they wondered—where exactly.

"The exile will be neither on Rizq nor Earth," he explained. "On the nearby planet of Mars there is water and an atmosphere. So, I have been considering the establishing of a processing station there. The planet's gravitational pull is less extensive than here on Earth and in the future it could prove to be to our advantage."

"I can take Alalu with me when I leave and drop him there when we pass the planet. Upon entering Mars' atmosphere we will release an aircraft with Alalu and some supplies in it. He will spend his final days alone, exile on a barren planet."

The decision was unanimous among the assembled judges and without delay, Anu appointed Nungal to pilot the ship on his return trip to Rizq. He informed everyone that Nungal would soon be returning to Earth with more teams of workers and then appointed Anzu to accompany them as a copilot and take charge of the Martian descent while they drop off Alalu.

The next morning, while Lord Anu was being ferried to the ship with Alalu and the rest of the crew, he turned to his youngest son. "Enlil," he said with a concerned tone. "You are going to need to build an adequate site to land our larger rocket ships, on firm, solid ground. We should also be making plans to utilize Mars as a way station." Enlil understood and he acknowledged his father's request.

As Lord Anu said goodbye to his sons, there was both joy and sorrow expressed between them. Upon their final farewell, Anu turned from his sons and boarded the large, golden spacecraft.

With his hands tied in front of him and limping, two very large guards escorted Alalu aboard the ship behind the king.

Enki exhaled. *So that would be the end of their struggle*, he thought. He had mixed feelings about Alalu. The attack on his father was unsettling enough, but knowing Alalu had hidden nuclear weapons on his ship was also rather disturbing. Did he bring them to protect himself? Were they a bargaining chip against Anu, or was it for some other dark purpose? Now, he would never know.

In a roar of orange rocket fire, the ascending spacecraft departed toward the heavens. When they had breached the Earth's atmosphere, Lord Anu watched the moon as they made their single pass around it and was quite captivated by its enigmatic presence. Upon passing the Earth satellite, they were now on their way to their first destination, Mars.

When they finally arrived at the red-hued planet, they made two passes around it. As they approached the surface, they could see the planets large mountains and valleys. They recognized the ancient pyramids next to the lake where Ea had once landed and they decided that it would be their drop point.

Inside the ship's hangar bay, they readied the aircraft that Alalu and Anzu would be using to descend to the planet's surface. It was Anzu's job to simply pilot the small craft, but he surprised them all when he made a most unexpected proposal.

"I will take Alalu to the surface, but I would like to stay on Mars to protect him until the end of his days. He and I share close blood ties, and when he dies from his internal wounds, I will bury him with honors that befit a—king."

"I will have made a name for myself and people will say that, against all odds, I was a companion to the exile king. They will speak of how I saw and faced unknown dangers on a strange alien world. They will know me as a hero until the end of times."

Alalu was overwhelmed by the sentiment, not knowing what to say—and Lord Anu was quite astounded by the brave proposal.

"Anzu," Anu said, "I will honor your wishes, and the next time a ship comes to Earth, they will stop at Mars and locate you. If you survive this world, when we establish our way station here, you will be appointed as its commander and be proclaimed Master of Mars."

Anzu bowed his head and Lord Anu decreed, "So be it."

The two were given high-tech space helmets, spacesuits, tools and food, and then ushered into their small aircraft. After the plane was released from the great ship's hangar bay, Anu and Nungal watched on their monitors as the craft got smaller and smaller while it made its descent to the Martian surface. Having taken care of their business on Mars, they were now ready to begin their long journey back to the Siriun home world of Rizq.

Alalu had ruled on Rizq for nine Shars and he had commanded on Earth for eight. His fate would ultimately be to die in exile on a strange planet in the ninth.

There was a joyous reception awaiting Lord Anu when he returned to the home world. It was only when he was finally alone with the council and the princes that he told them of Lord Alalu's attack and of the sentencing that followed. He explained that he wanted no animosity, pity or vengeance from them and the council was willing, even relieved, to put the issue behind them. With that said, they then began discussing the important tasks they would be undertaking. Anu instructed the council in their assignments as he outlined the great scope of his vision. A constant caravan of spaceships would carry gold from Earth, with way stations established on planets and moons along the way, Mars being the major one. He had also pointed out to them the plausibility of searching for gold on other worlds. The council members, the princes and the savants all took time to consider his ideas carefully as they weighed their options.

Finding salvation and promise in Lord Anu's plans, the savants and commanders consulted and perfected the celestial star charts as they prepared the coordinates needed for the important mission. New rocket ships were designed and added to the fleet, as top crew members were selected and trained in the vast array of various tasks that they would soon be needed for. There would be much to learn...

Enki and Enlil were beamed the transmission that informed them of what the council had agreed upon and what preparations on Earth were required of them. The discussions of what needed to be done were extensive, on top of the less-than-subtle implications from Rizq that it would be imperative that they hurry their preparations on Earth.

Enki appointed Alalgar to be the Overseer of the palace of Eridu during his trips to the Abzu to oversee what needed to be done there. After much contemplation and numerous sketches, he devised an ingenious machine called Earth Splitter to tunnel into the bowels of the Earth and another large tool that separated gold ore from rock and dirt he called The Crusher. Transmitting his designs back to Rizq, he had them custom fabricated to his specifications.

His next task was to calculate the multitude of tasks that were going to be required, and appoint the jobs accordingly.

As the Rizqian teams worked in Edin and the Abzu, they were not used to the quick passages of Earth's night and days, as it continued to cause them dizziness and physical discomfort. This, in turn, made their work much more difficult.

Enki consulted the Council back home and informed them about the crew's health and well-being. He told them of how his teams had been complaining more and more about the shortness of

Earth's daily cycles and its disorienting effects. Although the atmosphere on Earth was good, it was lacking in some things and too abundant in others. The crews had also been complaining about of the sameness of the food they were forced to eat, effectively eroding their morale even that much further.

In the meantime, Enlil had been busy surveying the lands by aircraft, taking measurements and making topographical accounts of valleys and plains in search of an ideal site for the massive landing pad he was planning to build. Finding himself afflicted by the heat of the sun, he was seeking out a cool place to build the permanent landing site. It was after flying over the snow-covered mountains to Edin's north, that he decided he favored them as the location for his spaceport's landing site. The tallest trees he had ever seen grew there in its Redwood Cedar Forests.

There, above a valley, Enlil had his teams flatten a mountain's entire surface with powerful laser beams. His men then quarried massive stones from a nearby hillside, and with the help of acoustic levitation devices, they were used in the construction of the enormous landing platform.

When the structure was completed, Enlil was quite pleased with the results and considered it to be truly a work of monumental proportions. The Rizqians Commanders commemorated the massive stone structure to Enlil and named it Baalbek—the Landing Place. They all agreed amongst themselves that the construction was a structure that would most certainly endure the test of time.

Enlil had also built a home for himself there in the Cedar Forest, on the crest of a nearby mountain. He utilized the massive cedar beams of the forest to build his personal mountain retreat. Once it was complete, large glass windows provided a vista view that looked out over the snow covered mountains and valleys below, and he named the elegant chalet—the Abode of the Northern Crest.

✦ ✦ ✦

On Rizq, a large, golden bell-shaped spacecraft was being loaded with the Earth Machines that Enki had designed, as well as brand new rocket ships, aircraft and supplies needed for the Earth operation. The new ship had been designed specifically for the important mission and Ninmah was put in command. She and her medical team of seventeen female scientists were among the group of fifty new crewmembers who would be coming to Earth. Trained in the arts of healing and aid to others, the treatment of ailments was one of Ninmah's specialties. She had been working on a remedy that would alleviate the harsh symptoms the crew had been experiencing on Earth and was bringing seeds for plants that would ultimately produce an elixir specially designed to counteract their discomfort.

✦ ✦ ✦

Often, while Enki was in meetings with the command in Eridu that concerned Edin's construction involving both him and Enlil, he mostly sat silent and let his brother, the legal heir, act as the supreme commander. Occasionally, an officer would address Enki with a command question by mistake; smoothly, Enki would wave in Enlil's direction and tell the officer to address the commander. It was obvious that Enlil was irritated when it happened. He wanted the complete respect of the crew, like Enki already had, but he was ever aware that he would have to earn it.

One day after such a meeting, Enlil asked Enki to stay in the room after the others had left, and he complied. "What is it, brother?" Enki asked, as he stood next to the console where Enlil was looking at charts.

"Now that the mining sites have been established and preparations to begin our excavations have commenced, the ships from home will be arriving soon with the new tools and supplies that we need for the mining operations. As you know, Ninmah and her team of medics will be among the new crew members that will be arriving with the first shipment."

"I see," Enki said. "It sounds like we are progressing as scheduled."

"Yes...we are," Enlil said, slowly. Enki sensed there was more to come.

"What is it you really want to tell me?" he asked bluntly.

Enlil looked away from what he was doing, but did not turn around. "It's about Ninmah," he said.

Enki tensed at her name being spoken. Immediately, images of her filled his mind. "Go on."

"As you know, I have been involved with our half sister..." Enlil said, "and she will be arriving soon with her team of female medical officers." He turned around to face Enki in order to gauge his reaction.

Enki just shrugged the comment off. He was also attracted to their younger sister, and at one time had been very much looking forward to the idea of being her spouse and having a son with her when his father had originally proposed the idea.

"You and I have an attachment, I believe," Enlil continued, "one of duty to our father's wishes."

And that's the only attachment, no brotherhood, Enki thought to himself. "Enlil, what are you trying to say about me and Ninmah?"

Enlil turned from the table to confront Enki face to face. "It was always foretold you and she would one day be joined in marriage to carry on the family lineage by the bearing of a son. That never happened. Ninmah and I...have something special together."

"I was never aware of that." Enki quietly responded.

Enlil found that rather hard to believe, considering that he and Ninmah had a son together, but he was relieved to finally discuss it openly.

"Really? Well, we do" Enlil said flatly, as he turned away from him to continue studying the charts that he had been looking at.

Without responding, Enki turned and walked out of the conference chamber, completely astounded by his younger brother's arrogance.

Chapter Three

The route to Earth from Sirius had been pre-encoded onto a Mae Stone crystal for Nungal's ship to follow. It was after a safe passage through the asteroid belt that a faint signal was picked up being transmitted from the surface of Mars.

"Commander Ninmah, there is a transmission coming from the approaching planet's surface. Its signature is *Rizqian*, my lady... it is coming from Anzu and Alalu," Nungal reported in astonishment.

When they reached Mars, they circled it slowly as they made their descent toward the planet's surface. Ninmah and Nungal followed the signal to the lakeshore near the ancient pyramids where Enki had originally landed. It was there that they realized that the beacon was coming from Prince Anzu's helmet.

By the lakeshore, they could see Anzu's body lying motionless in the dirt, possibly dead. Donning protective outerwear, Ninmah and Nungal left the ship to recover his body from the barren red wilderness. When they got to him, Ninmah knelt down and touched his helmet-covered face and then checked his life readings. They were faint. Taking a Pulser device from a pouch she carried with her, she aimed it at his heart. She then took out an Emitter Ray and radiated its crystal life force-giving energy over his entire body. Up to sixty attempts with both machines were made, and finally Anzu's eyes opened.

They carefully picked him up and escorted him back to the ship to be revived further. There, Ninmah gently gave him small amounts of water and a highly nourishing food substance to try to eat. After a while, he slowly began to recover.

"Anzu...?" Ninmah asked. "Can you tell us what has happened here...? Where is Alalu?"

Anzu looked at her for a moment as he gathered his strength to get up. "My lady...it would be best if I show you what has become of our vanquished king."

Standing up slowly, Anzu had Ninmah and Nungal take him to a great rock formation nearby that rose abruptly from the red dusty plains.

"This is where Lord Alalu now resides. His remains are buried inside a cave within this massive stone formation," he told them. "Our once noble king's death was horrifically painful and slow. Soon after the landing, Alalu began screaming in unrelenting pain as he spit up blood from his extensive internal injuries. Lord Alalu died in agony," Anzu said, softly. "Finding a cave in this great rock, I hid his body inside and covered the entranceway with stones."

They went to the cave and removed the barrier that Anzu had constructed. Inside they found that what remained of Alalu was now just a pile of decrepit bones. To Ninmah this turn of events was quite unsettling in its indignity. "For the first time in our recorded history, a king has died off-planet and was not buried on Rizq with ceremony and honor. Let him rest in peace for an eternity," she said softly. To effectively resolve this inglorious turn of events, Ninmah had an idea that would truly honor their fallen king.

Covering the cave entrance back up with stones, they left the burial tomb and returned to the ship. Once the supplies they had brought for the new way station were unloaded, Ninmah instructed Nungal to take one of the aircraft and carve Alalu's image into the great rock with the ship's laser beams. When he had finished, the great stone depicted the image of Alalu's face wearing his space helmet with its visor up.

From the ship's intercom, she announced to the crew, "May this monument of Lord Alalu forever gaze toward the planet of Rizq that he once ruled, and the Earth whose gold he had discovered. I proclaimed this officially in the name of my father, King Anu."

She turned away from the viewing monitor, "Anzu... you have survived the hardships of Mars, and Anu is prepared to keep his promise to you. I will leave twenty crewmembers here with you to begin building our processing station, and I assure you, there will be more crew arriving shortly. Ships from Earth will soon be bringing ore to Mars for its final stage of processing so that the purified gold can be loaded aboard larger ships to be transported back to the home world."

"There will be hundreds of crewmen stationed here by the time things are completed and you, Anzu, will be their commander," she told him proudly.

"I owe you my life, and my gratitude to Anu will be unlimited," he said as he laid back to rest.

After the equipment had been completely unloaded and the preliminary components of their base set up, Nungal prepared for departure and blasted off from the ancient landing site. Pushing through the Martian atmosphere, they made their way toward their final destination, planet Earth.

✦ ✦ ✦

Ninmah and her remaining team of fresh Anunaki recruits arrived on Earth after some brief prescheduled scanning of the moon's surface. Making two circuits around the blue planet to slow their large ships descent, they splashed down near Eridu, and the large golden vessel was moored at the newly built dock that now extended out into the ocean waters. The quay had been built on the gulf waters parallel to the shore to accommodate the newly arriving ships. Boats were now no longer needed.

When the craft's bay doors opened, Ninmah and her team proceeded down the large ramp that extended from the ship's massive holding area. The features of the female Anunaki were delicate, with thick gazelle-like horns that tapered back above their eyes and large beaks that tapered downward, being very birdlike in their appearance. They walked on raised haunches and as always, Enki was entranced by Ninmah's graceful movement and delicate beauty. When the team stepped off the ship, Enlil and Enki, who had been waiting for Ninmah's arrival, each took turns greeting their sister with a warm, loving embrace.

Ninmah returned her brothers greetings joyously and told them of how eager she was to tell them about recent events back home, and of what had happened during their stop on Mars. The two then locked arms with Nungal, as the gathered group of crewmen welcomed the new mix of male and female recruits with warm shouts and greetings.

Ninmah and the medical team she had brought with her were highly trained in the healing arts, and the crew stationed on Earth were in desperate need of their attention. This new atmosphere was causing them all a considerable amount of hardship and discomfort.

Enki was to inspect the new group that would be mining before they were to be sent to the mines of the Abzu. As he walked up and down the row of workers standing at attention, he noticed the slight differences between himself and them. As a member of the royal family, he had not had many encounters with the lower classes. Up close, they were shorter, less colorful, and their horns were nubby. Enki was aware that their lower status on the home world was what drove them to travel to this distant world for a chance at fortune, opportunity, even fame.

Whatever their exact reasons, they were here now and under his watch. His father had advised against telling them that Earth's atmosphere would be somewhat uncomfortable, that the hours would be long, and that there were risks of cave-ins within the bowels of the Earth, so Enki felt a little protective of the workers, knowing what they were about to face. There wasn't anything he could do about the conditions or the risk. All he could do was just hope that they would endure what was ahead of them the best they could.

"Everything seems to be in order, Commander Ennugi," he said.

"Have your crew board the transport shuttle to the Abzu and inform them that I will be joining them there shortly."

Under the watchful eye of Enki and Enlil, the precious cargo of the enormous golden ship was now carefully unloaded from its massive cargo bay. The newly arrived supplies consisted of equipment of all kinds, as well as the enormous Earth tools that Enki had designed. They had brought with them a multitude of provisions, including a wide range of seeds from Rizq that were to be planted within the Edin.

When the great ship had been completely unloaded, Ninmah was finally able to sit down with her brothers and tell them of the recent events on Rizq before she had left, of Alalu's death and burial on Mars, as well as the steps being taken to begin building their new processing station with Anzu as its commander.

"This *has* been a most interesting turn of events, sister," Enki uttered approvingly, but Enlil was bewildered and not so approving.

"Expanding our operations to Mars is thoroughly impractical! What, exactly, is the point of this?"

"Brother," Ninmah said to him, "Father's word is unalterable. But don't worry about that right now. Look...I have brought relief from the Earth maladies." She took out a bag of seeds from a pouch.

"When these seeds are planted, they will produce a variety of fruit bearing plants. It is from the essence of these plants that we will produce a powerful healing elixir."

"When our workers drink it, their mood will be elevated and their ailments will be alleviated," she told them. "But the seeds will need to be planted in a cool place with warm sunlight and water."

"I know of the *perfect* place...," Enlil said. "I can show it to you right now actually." He took Ninmah by the hand and they bid Enki farewell. He then escorted her to his private aircraft and from Eridu, they flew to Baalbek—the Landing Place in the snow-covered mountains of the Cedar Forest, to his Abode of the Northern Crest.

Once the two commanders had left, Ninmah's team of female

medics were ordered to gather their belongings and they boarded the shuttlecrafts that would take them to their new medical facility assignments.

✦ ✦ ✦

On route to Baalbek, Ninmah looked out over the lands and she liked what she saw very much. "This world is quite unique...and I must say that I truly admire all that you have achieved here," she told Enlil softly.

"Well, if you like what you have seen so far, just wait until you see my grandest achievement yet...the Landing Site of Baalbek."

As Enlil set his aircraft down on the giant stone platform, Ninmah was definitely impressed with the enormous structure. From there, the two siblings wasted no time and quickly made their way to Enlil's mountain retreat. Once inside his chalet, Enlil embraced Ninmah in his arms and they began to grope each other's bodies with an unbridled passion.

"Oh, my sister...my beloved," he said as he lifted her onto a nearby countertop, and the two made love as if they had been ravaged by prolonged hunger. Enlil was reserved though, as he retained his essence when he did not release his seed into her.

Ninmah believed that what she shared with Enlil was special. However, she did feel something for Enki as well, but she would not allow her mind to go down that path. She whispered softly in Enlil's ear how she had brought words from their son, Ninutra.

"The adventurous young prince is ready to join you on Earth, my lord," she said softly as she nuzzled his ear. "Let him come and stay here."

Enlil gently pulled away and stood with his back to her as he stared blankly out the large front room window, looking down at the white mountains below them. He was deep in thought. She put her hand on his shoulder. "What is it, my lord?" she asked.

Enlil paused before he spoke, "We are here for a reason."

Ninmah was confused for a moment. "Of course, I know that, Enlil."

"Do you really?" he asked, with an abruptness that she was not expecting.

Ninmah took her hand away, startled. Realizing what he had done, Enlil turned around to clasp her hands in his own.

"I'm sorry, Ninmah, I do not mean to be harsh with you. I'm just concerned about how all of this is going to turn out. Here we are... light years away from our home world, coming into another world's environment and exploiting it for our own gains.

"If the creators of this paradise world, the Draco, were to ever hear of how we were taking their gold... it would surely create war between our two great races. We believe we have a noble purpose here, but do we have the right to do this?"

Ninmah squeezed Enlil's hand to reassure him. "Yes, my lord, we very much have the right. The Draco haven't been on this planet for eons. Who knows what other worlds they must be off creating?"

She paused as she looked for a reaction. "Do not trouble yourself over this, my lord. Our people have existed for millennia, having developed one of the most powerful technologies in the known universe. Now our future is threatened. We must survive, any way that we can. And if that means we come to another world and mine some resources that obviously aren't being used, well, that's just how it has to be." She shrugged. "We still have much to learn and achieve through our great society—we can not fail."

"Thank you, Ninmah, for reminding me of our goals," Enlil seemed relieved. "We are indeed doing the right thing. The main point is to ensure that we make as little impact on this world as possible, then one day, we and our future generations can return home." He went back to the window. "I do have many ideas for this world, beyond Edin and I would very much like to have my son here to assist me. There will be much to do. In the future I envision five great cities, each with their own purpose, all interconnected within the Edin."

Ninmah smiled. "This plan... sounds most spectacular, my lord."

A spaceship from Rizq was arriving at Baalbek with supplies and more new recruits, just as Ninmah, Enlil and some of his crew were going down into the nearby valley to plant the seeds that she had brought with her from Rizq. The group separated and planted the many varieties of seeds with special, high-tech planting wands that had been brought from the home world. When they had finished, Enlil and Ninmah boarded an aircraft, left Baalbek and made their way back to the Palace in Eridu.

On their way back, Enlil showed his sister Edin's landscape and the parameters of its estate as he explained the extent of his plans to her.

"I have laid out for us a construction of monumental proportions. Not far from Eridu, where the dry land begins, is where I will construct our operations center. Built on the banks of the mighty river Euphrates, it will be known as—Laarsa.

"We will then build a Twin City—Lagash, on the other side of Edin. Between these great cities, a city devoted to healing will be established. It shall be *your* city Ninmah, and it will be named Shurubak—the Healing City. At Edin's very center, a fourth city and transmissions tower will be built. Being the hub of our central command, it will be known as Nibru-ki—the Bond that Crosses the Stars."

"Nibru-ki will be the home of a tall communications tower that will scan the celestial heavens and all the lands. It will be in this command center that the Mae Stones running all our operations will be housed. With Eridu included…there will ultimately be a total of five cities that will facilitate our operations within the Edin."

As they were looking at the plans that had been recorded into the Mae crystal, Ninmah noticed another group of documents that he had neglected to show her. "Enlil…what are these files regarding alternatives to Anu's plans for the way station on Mars?" He reached over and pressed a crystal panel on the console and his plans for a refinement center with a landing facility large enough for the largest of Siriun spacecraft directly from Rizq, came up within the center of the large crystal monitor they were using.

"There is just absolutely no need to create a refinement station on Mars!" he told her.

Ninmah now understood a little better. "My brother, your plans for the five cities are magnificent and I am especially grateful for the creation of the healing city of Shurubak as my abode. But Enlil, do *not* transgress beyond Lord Anu's plan. The High Council may take offense to your overstepping the boundaries of your authority."

"Ninmah, I have been thinking about that, and you actually make a very valid point. You are right...I should no longer pursue this line of thinking." He turned off the holographic images and looked at her. "You are truly as wise as you are beautiful, my dear sister."

Meanwhile, Enki had been doing extensive surveys over the Abzu by aircraft. Often while measuring and surveying the lands, he would take mental note of its richness—bursting with life, perfect in its fullness. Having already pinpointed the exact location of the site where they would be entering the Earth, Enki had now begun to seek out a spot to build a command center that would be his abode and scientific research center.

With many mighty rivers running through the Abzu regions, it was in a place that accommodated these flowing waters that he decided to build his personal dwelling and botanical laboratories.

Back at the site where they would be digging into the Earth— the Place of Deepness—the teams were busy setting up the massive, specially designed machines, Earth Splitter and The Crusher. The enormous machines would produce extremely large payloads of gold bearing ore that would be loaded onto large aircraft and carried to the Landing Place of Baalbek in the Cedar Mountains. The teams there would transfer the shipments to rocket ships and send them to the orbiting space platforms for the ore's initial refinement in a completely weightless environment. The large amounts of waste would be dispersed into space and simply burn up on its re-entry into the atmosphere. The gold would then be sent to Mars for its final stage of purification and ultimately, be sent to Rizq, where it would be turned to a fine dust and dispersed into the atmosphere.

More and more recruits from the home world were now arriving on Earth, some being assigned to Edin and some to the Abzu. In time, the constructions of the three outposts Laarsa, Lagash and Shurubak were completed. Ninmah took her residence in the Healing City of Shurubak with a host of young female healers. In Nibru-ki, Enlil had the construction well underway for the building of his transmission tower and central command center. Although tedious, Enki would travel back and forth between the Abzu and Edin on a regular basis in order to supervise the construction of the gleaming new cities and still watch over their mining operations.

On Mars, the construction of the base was nearly complete, as new crew members were arriving for duty regularly. For two celestial rotations of Rizq, the construction continued on Earth and when all was ready, Lord Anu gave a speech addressed to the entire crew from their home world via holographic transmission to all their settlements. It was on their seventh day, their traditional day of rest, that they all assembled in their places of dwelling and heard the words of Lord Anu.

Near Eridu, in the palace compound of Laarsa, many of the elite assembled within the lush, plant-filled, tan marble hall with its many waterfalls and unique water features that ran through it. Enlil stood at the front of the great reception hall with Ninmah by his side. Next to Lady Ninmah stood Alagar and the team of young female officers. Abgal, now commander of Baalbek, was also in attendance, accompanied by his crew and the teams that had been assigned to work the orbiting refinement platforms.

Down in the Abzu, Enki was also assembled with his teams. Accompanied by his vizier, Isimud and his pilot, Nungal, he stood on a raised outdoor podium as he looked out over the group with proud nobility.

On Mars, the team also stood assembled at attention with their proud commander Anzu. Six hundred on Earth and three hundred on Mars were gathered. They all listened to the words of their king Lord Anu that day.

"My brethren, you are the saviors of our world! The fate of all is in your hands! You will forever be recorded in the history books as glorious heroes.

"In honor of your great achievements, those of you on Earth shall henceforth be known as the Anunaki—Those Who Have Come to Earth from the Stars! In accordance... the crews on Mars shall be known as the Igigi—Those Who Observe and See!

All that is required is ready... let the gold start coming and let Rizq be saved!"

Chapter Four

Deep within the jungles of the Abzu, Enki had created a highly advanced botanical and science laboratory for himself that he named Ebineru—the House of Life. Located over a mighty river, one of the most prominent features of this large glass and stainless steel research center was the tube-like glass tunnels underneath it that went off in many different directions into the rainforest jungles. The clear observation tunnels went down through the river waters and branched out into the surrounding jungle, just below the ground's surface.

These clear tunnels would allow Enki and his teams to enter the rainforest jungles at various points and remain virtually undetected while observing the ways of the natural habitat. Enki wanted to study all of Earth's life forms to understand its secrets of life and death. He had furnished Ebineru with all manner of tools and equipment that he had specially designed and shipped to him from Rizq. It was indeed a most wondrous place to study and observe nature.

Walking the bright, tubular hallways within the House of Life, Enki came to the Medical Center. Through the glass he could see Ninmah in her lab coat discussing some documents on her hand-held screen with an assistant. She noticed him standing there, and as the assistant left, she gestured for him to enter the lab.

"Enki, what a pleasant surprise. Are you here to pick up your mining crew?"

Enki nodded. He stared at her for a moment without saying anything. Ninmah looked at him with concern. "I'm sorry, aside from the elixir, there's not much we can do for them in this atmosphere. Our regenerative sciences are intrinsically designed for the physiology of the noble bloodlines only and the masks we've designed don't work very well in damp, underground environments. I am still working on some other design prototypes though—"

"Ninmah..." Enki interrupted, but was then silent.

He wanted her badly...but their lives were based on order and tradition. Even though their own father had crushed tradition with his coup...and they *had* already developed an intimate relationship, Enki had to push thoughts of passion out of his mind. He needed to be the logical one and stay focused on the important tasks of the mission.

✦ ✦ ✦

One morning, in the Cedar Forest, while walking in the cool shade of the cedar trees, Enlil happened upon a group of Ninmah's young female recruits who had been assigned to the Landing Place of Baalbek. They were bathing in the cool waters of a mountain stream. As he watched them, Enlil became enchanted by the grace and beauty of one young female in particular. Her name was Sud, and he called her away from the rest of the group.

"You are looking most ravishing today Sud," Enlil said as he looked at her with hungry eyes. "Please... Come with me to my chalet. You simply *must* try the elixirs that we have created from the home world plants grown here on Earth," he said to her, entirely captivated by her beauty. As not to offend the prince, the young recruit accepted his request.

Once at his chalet, the two partook of Enlil's special elixir. Shortly thereafter, with no subtlety to his advances, Enlil propositioned Sud to have sexual relations with him.

"My lord...I am a virgin, and my vagina is much too small for you," she replied bashfully.

Dismayed with her response, he pulled back a bit. "Well then... at least give me a kiss," he told her.

"No, my lord...even a kiss would be inappropriate. I have never been kissed before," she replied timidly. Enlil just laughed as he embraced and kissed her anyway. Taking advantage of Sud, he had sex with her despite her unwillingness...and it was with no reserve whatsoever that he poured his seed into her.

Sud reported Enlil's actions to Ninmah and she was outraged. Calling him at his office, his holographic image appeared within the domed crystal monitor on her desk. He was sitting comfortably in a spiked command chair within his misty, plant-filled office at Baalbek.

"Ninmah, my dear, hello," he said.

She had no patience for him whatsoever. "Enlil! How dare you lust after one of the youngest of my cadets? You are...immoral!"

Enlil said nothing as he stared back at her blankly. Ninmah told him with narrowed eyes, "Mark my words, Enlil, you *will* stand before the High Council for this and be held accountable for your lecherous deeds," and she abruptly shut off the transmission.

In the gathered presence of fifty Anunaki, the court of the Seven Who Judge assembled, with Enki seated centrally in the highest chair.

"Enlil...son of Anu, the High Council has reviewed your case and based on your behavior, we decree that you be banished from all cities for a period of two years and sent to a remote wilderness, he announced." The council had spoken...Enlil's immediate fate had been sealed.

Accepting the decision with a subtle arrogance, Enlil was silent as they took him away. It was Abgal that was subsequently assigned to transport Enlil to this land of exile, but when they began the journey, he surprised the banished commander and went in a completely different direction, taking him to a place amidst foreboding mountains and jagged cliffs.

Landing their aircraft on a rocky crag, Abgal finally explained his plan. "My lord...this is to be your place of exile, and it is not by chance that I have chosen it—for Enki has hidden a *secret* here. In a nearby cave, he has hidden some nuclear weapons that we had discovered onboard Alalu's ship."

"If you report this to the council, my lord," he said, "you could surely regain your freedom."

Abgal then bid Enlil farewell, assuring him that he would return before long with fresh provisions. In the windy blast of the ship's thrusters, the banished Anunaki prince was left alone on the rocky cliff, next to the cave in the secret place.

Back in Edin, Sud confides in her commander that she has recently become aware that she is pregnant with Enlil's child. Taking into consideration the pregnancy's full regal implications, Ninmah immediately tells Enki of what has happened, as he was now in command of the Edin. He contacts his father on the home world at once and informs him of the full details of the recent turn of events.

Lord Anu tells the Seven Who Judge to summon Sud and ask her if she would be willing to take Lord Enlil as her spouse, and it was with no uncertainty that she graciously accepts and tells them yes.

When Abgal returned to Enlil's place of exile to tell him of Sud's acceptance of espousal, they were both in agreement that this course of action was indeed much more beneficial than what they had been considering previously.

When they get back to Edin, Enki and Ninmah give Enlil a complete pardon and Sud becomes Enlil's official spouse. With her new title, she is also given a new name...Ninlil—Lady of the Command. In time, she gives birth to their son and they name him Nannar—the Bright One. The child is an official royal heir, the first Anunaki Royal to be born on the alien planet of Earth.

In the aftermath of his brother's scandal, Enki discreetly suggests to Ninmah that she abandon her infatuation with Enlil and return to the Abzu to be with him.

She took a moment as she reflected on the dazzling silver and glass science complex of Ebineru, complete with its lapis lazuli inlayed trim work that he knew she loved. Ninmah was taken by his request, considering that it was true, she *had* become very disillusioned by Lord Enlil's seductive charms as of late... so, she agrees to go the Abzu to be with Enki.

When Ninmah arrived, Enki held her and expressed his true feelings towards her. He told her how he still loved her and that they were meant to be together. He caressed her gently and the two of them made passionate love. When the heat of their love-making climaxed, Enki poured his seed into her as he cried out, "Oh Ninmah, give me a son...!"

Ninmah did become pregnant, and in time she gave birth to a beautiful baby girl whom they name Ninkasi. When they were looking at her, Ninmah and Isimud told Enki to kiss the child, but he refused to due to his frustration in that he had very much wanted a son.

Enki took Ninmah into his arms again and made love to her again, and once more, she bore him a female child. Angrily, he cried out, "A son, Ninmah! I *must* have a son!" He took her again, but by then Ninmah had had enough and she uttered curses of physical ailments upon him for his brash behavior.

When the Anunaki in Edin summoned Isimud and told him that Ninmah's assistance was needed back in Shurubak, Enki was in truth quite relieved. Ninmah's subtle curses had actually been taking quite a toll on his physical health as of late. With raised arms, he exclaimed to Isimud, "Yes...I know. Be assured old friend, I will distance myself from Ninmah and I will abandon this obsession of conceiving an heir to our kingdom with her!" This was indeed what was needed to effectively remove his current ailments, and the curse that she had placed upon him was lifted.

So Ninmah returned to Edin, never to be espoused—her father's command fulfilled.

Enki consoled himself: when Enlil sends his son Nannar's daughter, Erishkigal, down to the Abzu from Nibru-ki to run the facility's astronomical and Earth monitoring station, he accompanies her on the trip. It was on route to the Abzu that Enki makes his true intensions clear to her, and he seduces Erishkigal. She becomes pregnant with his child and in time, gives him a son whom they name Ningishzida—Thoth.

Chapter Five

In the Abzu, gold ore was being brought to the surface from deep within the veins of the Earth. The mix of dirt and ore was loaded onto airships that would carry it to the Landing Place of Baalbek, in the Cedar Mountains. There, it would be loaded aboard enormous rocket ships and sent to their orbiting space platforms for initial refinement, before it was sent to Mars for its final refinement. From Mars, pure gold bars were sent to Rizq where they would be turned to a fine dust and distributed into their upper atmosphere. Slowly, the breach in the Heavens was healing; slowly Rizq was saved.

In Edin, the five cities were being perfected. The massive estate had been enclosed by a force field of thin, orange fire that completely surrounded it. It was then seeded with many strange and wondrous varieties of plant, insect, and animal life direct from Rizq to create a highly unique alien jungle eco-system. The plant life was aggressive and it soon created a thick rainforest jungle, teaming with life. Enki rebuilt Eridu and constructed a monumental palace in its place that looked very much like a giant, flattened chrome teardrop. Surrounded by water, many tall gleaming silver spires accentuated its parameter, while three long causeways spanned from the land to its main entryways.

Enki contacted the home world and requested his spouse Damkina and his son Marduk come to Earth to live in Eridu. As Ea had received his new title name Enki—Lord of Earth, upon his wife's arrival on Earth, she was given a new title name as well. She was now to be known as Ninki—Lady of Earth. There, in the gleaming Water Palace, Enki taught them his knowledge of the Earth and all its many wondrous mysteries.

✦ ✦ ✦

In Edin's central city of Nibru-ki, Enlil was putting the finishing touches on his high-tech surveillance tower and transmissions base. Certainly, the most prominent feature of this immense complex was the tall slender, black chrome transmission tower that rose from its center. Perched at its lofty tip, the tower supported a large, pointed dome shaped control room. The complex of Nibru-ki was truly a magnificent sight to behold. From this lofty command center, transmissions were now able to reach *all* settlements…on Earth, Mars, and Rizq.

Tall, thin, black chrome surveillance spires, flared at their bases, were constructed and strategically placed throughout the grounds of Edin. The small spherical camera balls at their lofty tips would enable them to monitor virtually all of the enormous complex.

As the Five Cities were being perfected, a monorail system was built that ran in all directions throughout the lands of Edin's vast estate. It connected the Five Great Cities and gave the Anunaki access to various key points within its well-manicured, alien jungles. From this central city of Nibru-ki, all systems of communications could be governed from its tall, black Space Needle, including celestial observations. Within its lofty, crown like chamber, the radar systems could now monitor the entire planet, as well as Edin's extensive estate, making any unwanted approach virtually impossible to escape detection.

In a special room, deep within the complex's core, the celestial passages of the stars' and the processions of Earth's fellow planets were charted and recorded onto a series of multicolored quartz Mae Stone crystals. The crystal shards were housed in tablets set into a small table located in the center of the room, while the computer consoles on the walls around them hummed quietly in their soft multicolored glow. Now, whenever he would come to this private chamber, Enlil felt a great sense of satisfaction knowing that he was able to monitor virtually all Anunaki activity on Earth—in the Edin as well as the Abzu.

Chapter Six

Among the unrest from the Siriun worker force, the grumbling was the loudest from the Igigi, on Mars. When the last Igigi team had arrived to transport ore back to the Martian refinement centers, they made it very clear that they wanted to be able to stay on Earth a short while for some much needed rest and relaxation.

In Enlil's personal office in Nibru-ki, he was in conference with Enki in Eridu and Lord Anu on Rizq in a three-way conversation via hologram.

"My sons, the Igigi *must* continue to adhere to their production schedule," Anu told them. "We have no time for leisure-based activities." He was very adamant. "We must bring Anzu to Earth for a conference to discuss the matter."

"The two of you will show him the extent of our labors in the Abzu and in the Edin. It will be through this that he will come to gain a more complete understanding of the process, in hopes that it will effectively justify a restraint on their demands."

✦ ✦ ✦

When Anzu arrived at the complex of Nibru-ki to explain the Igigi's complaint, Enlil made a point not see him right away and purposefully kept him waiting. Although Lord Anu had ordered Anzu be shown all operations, Enlil was still uncomfortable with the idea so he stalled the meeting. When Enki was informed of this, he contacted Enlil, his holographic image appearing within a large crystalline monitor on Enlil's desk.

"Enlil, Anzu has been waiting for you to debrief him on the details of our operations. Why have you been keeping him?"

Enlil turned and addressed him with a very serious look on his face. "As you know brother, Anzu was Alalu's close relative and it was our father, King Anu, who had him exiled. And *now* he incites the Igigi into making demands? Surely, it is I—not Anzu—who gives the orders on this mission."

Enlil believed that he alone controlled the entire Earth operation; Anzu and the Igigi must obey, not challenge him.

"Yes Enlil," Enki said. "As this may certainly be the case…these orders come from father. He feels that it is essential in this situation that you explain the gold mining, refinement and transport systems to him."

"Well…all right. I shall do as he wishes," Enlil said, after mulling it over for a little while. He raised his eyes and looked at Enki. "I will debrief Anzu here. Afterwards, you take him to the Abzu where he can witness the toil in the mines and experience their sludge-ridden work environments for himself. Maybe *then* he will see things more clearly."

Enki met up with Anzu and they traveled to the Abzu together. After a complete tour of the mining facilities and Enki's House of Life, they returned to the Water Palace of Eridu. Enlil contacted Anzu there and invited him back to Nibru-ki where he was prepared to show him the Hallowed Chamber where all command operations were housed.

When Anzu arrived at Nibru-ki shortly thereafter, Enlil still had his reservations but allowed him to enter the innermost sanctuary, deep within the large complex. The small control room was dimly lit by the glowing, multicolored Mae Stones set into a computer table in the center of the room. Once inside, he explained to Anzu the particular purpose linked to each differently colored Mae Stone crystal. The blue crystal shards governing their medical operations, the green—botanicals, yellow shards—satellite communications, orange shards—security, red crystals—weapons, and the purple Mae Stones—governed all machinery. The clear Mae crystals contained information that ran all the rest of the other various components within their Earth operations.

After his tour of the heart of their operations in Nibru-ki, Anzu was shuttled aboard a monorail tram that carried him to the rest of the Five Cities, where he was shown the full extent of their facilities and the operations within them.

Upon their return to Nibru-ki, Enki finally brought up the issue of the Igigi demands.

"So, tell me Anzu..." Enki asked, "Do you now grasp the extent of how much of our operation is depending on you and your Igigi's continual transportation of gold ore? There is simply no time to be spared for rest and relaxation excursions."

Anzu just looked at him blankly. "Although I must admit, my lord, that while the extent of our operations here on Earth is quite impressive, it is of no consolation to the excessive demands put on my Igigi workers. They get very little time off, and the time they do have off is spent in an inhospitable, barren environment. I can tell you, my lord... there is very little leisure to be had on Mars."

Enki looked down and gave a heavy sigh. He remembered how desolate the red planet had been, and he could not imagine having to actually be stationed there. It was then that he had come to terms with the idea that Anzu was probably right.

"When it comes right down to it...I have to agree with you Anzu, Mars is truly insufferable," he said. "The best I can do for you is submit a proposal for the necessary measures that will need to be taken to accommodate relief for your Igigi workers. Upon our return to Nibru-ki, we will speak with Enlil about arranging the necessary preparations."

A prince among princes, Anzu was of a high royal lineage, but evil intentions filled his heart when they returned to the mission's headquarters of Nibru-ki. Anzu had been speaking with Enlil's youngest son Nannar recently about the Mae Stone crystals that ran the Edin, and they had been secretly plotting to steal them. With the stones in their possession, Nannar would easily be able to challenge his older brother Ninutra for command as Enlil's successor, so that he would one day take over and control the mission on Earth.

But Anzu had plans of his own and wanted to take away Enlil's title now, so that he would rule the Anunaki on Earth, as well as the Igigi on Mars.

Back in Nibru-ki, unsuspecting of his treachery, Enlil allows Anzu to be stationed temporarily at the inner sanctuary's entrance while he leaves the complex briefly to go for a cooling swim in a nearby lake.

Once he is alone at his post, Anzu quietly slips into the control room and from the small table in the center of the room, he removes the tablet of Mae Stone crystals that run the Spaceport and Cities of the Edin. Placing them in a small bag, he quickly makes his way to the facilities landing concourse and hijacks one of the military aircraft in Enlil's fleet. At gunpoint, he orders Abgal to fly him to the Landing Place of Baalbek in the Cedar Mountains, where the rebellious Igigi are eagerly anticipating his arrival.

When Anzu lands his stolen aircraft at Baalbek, loud cries of assured victory among the Igigi boldly declare him king of Earth and Mars as they take over the facility.

Back in Nibru-ki and all over Edin the power begins to shut down. The hum of machines stop, lights go out and computers shut down. Communication between Earth and Rizq is severed.

When Enlil returns to Nibru-ki he is absolutely astonished and completely overwhelmed by the treacherous act of broken trust.

Enraged, the first thing he does is contact Enki on his small, personal handheld communication device.

"Enki…my suspicions were correct! Anzu is not to be trusted. *He* is the reason all of our cities have shut down!" he snarled angrily. "Anzu has stolen the Mae Stones of Nibru-ki!"

"You know I have *never* been convinced of the authenticity of his bloodlines claim to our throne," he added indignantly as he shook his fist with rage.

✦ ✦ ✦

In Nibru-ki, they assembled all of the Anunaki commanders where they are able to consult Lord Anu through a patched signal transmitted from one of their parked spacecraft.

"Anzu must be seized and the Mae Stones returned immediately!" Anu shouted, his image looking out over the group. "Who among you can insure his capture?"

The leaders knew that with the stones in his possession, Anzu was virtually invincible. Encouraged by his mother Ninmah, Ninutra stepped forward from the assembled group.

"My lords…I will be Enlil's commando warrior, and I will capture Anzu."

They all expressed their approval and Ninutra's proposal was accepted. Now that it was established that he would be the one bringing Anzu to justice, Enlil and Enki set to prepare him for his confrontation through a masterful strategy and some unique weaponry. Enlil had his son's aircraft equipped with a powerful, multi-headed missile that he was to fire only at a very close wing-to-wing range.

Piloting the small, delta-winged flyer, Ninutra made his way to Baalbek where the traitorous fugitive Anzu was holed up inside of the command center within the hillside of one the Landing Site's nearby mountains.

On his approach, Ninutra contacted Anzu via hologram, and his image appeared within a crystal dome inside of Baalbek's command center. "Anzu! You must give up the Mae Stones, release the hostages, and turn yourself in *immediately*," he commanded.

"What bold arrogance," Anzu mocked. "With the Mae Stone crystals in my possession, you could *never* defeat me." Ninutra fired laser shots at the hideout, but they were deflected off a force field.

The lasers did no damage, but the commander was a nuisance and Anzu wanted him dealt with. Ninutra continued with the assault on the hideout and his ploy worked; Anzu rose to the challenge in another fighter craft to "easily take care of the insignificant, young Lieutenant."

Unknown to Anzu, Enki had instructed Ninutra to use a whirlwind device against him. He had it installed to create a dust storm that would blind Anzu and disorient his senses.

From an opening in the side of the hill, Anzu's plane quickly rose to the challenge and he flew wing to wing with the small delta-winged fighter craft. Looking out his window, he could see Ninutra clearly. Anzu shouted to the young pilot through the holographic transmission, "You insolent fool...! This battle will be your destruction!"

Quickly, Ninutra activates the whirlwind device that effectively creates a powerful dust storm, catching Anzu off guard and obscuring his visual orientation. Losing sight of his target, Anzu leaves the underside of his wing exposed. When Ninutra fires the special multi-headed missile, Anzu's wing is engulfed in flames, effectively damaging his craft's steering mechanism.

Ninutra's heart beat heavily in his chest as he watched the enemy aircraft spin to the ground and explode in a burst of flames.

After Anzu lost control of his aircraft, he had ejected and parachuted safely to the ground where Ninutra went and found him to take him into custody. Upon his capture, Ninutra confiscated the tablets of stolen crystals from the small rucksack that Anzu carried slung around his shoulder.

At Baalbek, the Igigi had all witnessed the events as they transpired, and groveled, kneeling at Ninutra's feet when he returned to the Landing Place with his prisoner. When he regained control of the Command Center, Ninutra released the captive Abgal and the Anunaki workers, and immediately sent word to Anu and Enlil that his mission had been successful and that the Maes were safely retrieved.

When Ninutra returned to Nibru-ki, the tablets were reinstalled within the Master Control chamber. The lights in Edin came back on, as the glow and soft hum of the crystals refilled the small, mission control room.

Anzu was imprisoned, and ultimately taken before the Seven Who Judge for his trial. The High Council that would be sentencing him consisted of Enlil, his son Nannar, Enlil's spouse Ninlil, Enki, his son Marduk, Enki's spouse Damkina, and Ninmah.

When all were assembled Ninutra spoke to the court of the evil deeds Anzu had committed. "There is absolutely no justification to fit this crime," he told them. "The penalty should be death."

From the podium of judges, Marduk countered the statement. "The Igigi have the right to have a place to rest on Earth established for them," he said.

Enlil felt that this was completely irrelevant. "Anzu put every single Igigi and all Anunaki in danger by this evil, treacherous deed!"

Anzu glanced briefly at Nannar with a subtle pleading in his eyes in hopes that he would say something, but Nannar in no way wanted to be implicated in what had transpired. He remained silent, as he discretely tried to avoid any kind of direct eye contact with the accused.

Enki agreed with Enlil, and so did Ninmah. "This evil must be extinguished!" she said forcefully.

The Seven Who Judge were all in agreement upon a death by execution sentence for Anzu, and with a killing ray, his life was quickly extinguished. After the execution, however, there was some debate on what they should do with the body.

"His remains should be left to the vultures," Ninutra posed with an indifferent lack of sentiment.

"No, he should be buried in the cave on Mars next to Alalu," Enki said. "They were from the same ancestral seed. Marduk, you speak for the Igigi, do you not? Maybe you should be the one to take the body to Mars and take command there as his successor."

"So be it," Enlil said. "You shall present the corpse as an example. See that the Igigi *obey* their orders, or they themselves will end up as Anzu has," he told him sternly.

Enlil's suspicions had been raised by Anzu's strange behavior toward Nannar, so to insure his oldest son's sovereign authority, he took a moment to make all the commanders swear Ninutra as his successor as commander on Earth.

With Anzu's body in his ship's storage hold, Marduk was sent to the facility on Mars to command. Efficient in his duties, in time he was able to see to the Igigi's well-being and he effectively improved the working conditions there.

Chapter Seven

On Earth, the Anunaki toiled. In Edin, the work was consistent, and in the Abzu, it was backbreaking and consistent. The crews often complained that the work was overwhelming and that the sustenance rations they were forced to call food was terrible, almost insulting even. The Earth's short cycles were still causing them dizziness and discomfort, but the workers were only given small rations of the elixirs that alleviated the negative symptoms. Not only were the extractions extremely tedious to procure and highly addictive, it ultimately proved to be very harmful to the nervous system.

Enki scheduled a meeting with Enlil in Nibru-ki to discuss a solution that would more effectively alleviate the harsh effects that the stay on Earth was having on the crew. Deep within the chamber of the Maes at Nibru-ki, he and Enlil discussed the problem over the soft glow of the central table of multicolored crystals.

"Enlil…the stays here on Earth are too prolonged for the working class," Enki said. "The side effects are now impacting our production levels. We must come up with a solution soon!"

"I've known that the work has always been difficult under the negative effects of the Earth atmosphere," Enlil said. "But I was unaware that the recent drop in production was directly related to the actual incapacitation of our workforce. Something will definitely need to be done soon, before our whole operation begins to suffer."

The two called on Ninmah for her professional medical opinion, and when Enlil brought her hologram onscreen for conference, she was looking very tired herself. He and Enki glanced at one another with a surprised concern when they saw how haggard her demeanor had become. "Greetings, sister are you well?" said Enki. She nodded to the affirmative. "Well, as you know, our workforce has been suffering greatly from long-term exposure to this Earth atmosphere. We can no longer rely on drugs to mask these harsh side effects."

Ninmah took a deep breath and looked at them. "The fact is, since the gold we harvest here must be sent to Rizq as quickly as possible, new workers more often would certainly relieve the pressure being put on the workforces on hand," she told them. "My son, prince Ninutra, has recently presented to me a surprisingly viable solution." She then brought up the prerecorded presentation he had made for them within their crystalline video monitor.

Ninutra, well versed in the science of ore refinement from inner Earth, suggested in the proposal that a new city be created that could initially refine the ore prior to transport directly to Mars for its final refinement. With the gold smelted and partially refined, each rocket ship would be able to carry more gold, as well as have additional room for Anunaki workers to return to Rizq.

After his presentation, Enlil, Enki and Ninmah all came to the conclusion that it was indeed an exceptional plan.

✦ ✦ ✦

The council on Rizq accepted Ninutra's proposal, but when Lord Anu gave his final approval for the new complex, Enlil insisted that they build it within the Edin. The council was in concurrence and the new facility was built in Edin near Lagash with specially designed materials brought to them from Rizq. When it was completed, they equipped the large complex with a multitude of unique refinement tools, also sent from the home world.

There was a coronation ceremony and they named the new facility Bad-Tibira—the City Where the Ores Are Processed.

Ninutra was made commander of Bad-Tibira and the flow of gold to Rizq was quickened, effectively easing some of the burden on the Anunaki workers. It had been a much longer tour than anyone had expected. Old crew members who had come to Earth in the beginning of the mission, were finally going back home to Rizq—Alagar, Abgal, Nungal and many others.

The newcomer replacement recruits sent from the home world were young and eager Cadets who were looking for adventure. They grew up in a world where the atmosphere had been healing and imminent doom wasn't hanging above their heads. They sought gold and the challenge of conquering a new world. Because of the fact that they had never been told, they were all very unaware of how harsh this alien environment would actually be. The new crews were delivering the gold ore on time to Bad-Tibira, and the refined gold ore was being sent back to Rizq more efficiently...but the newcomers were not pleased with the un-expected working conditions, and they soon rebelled.

✦ ✦ ✦

Enki was too busy studying a full spectrum of Earth life in Ebineru to notice the unrest brewing among the new mining recruits. Lately, he had been focusing the whole of his attentions on the Abzu and all that lived and grew within it.

Enki had spoken with his son Ningishzida—an expert in genet-ics—and suggested that he transfer to the Abzu jungles from his assignment in Nibru-ki to assist him in his current studies. Enki felt that he would be an invaluable asset in helping him discover the secrets of life and death on Earth so that the Anunaki could over-come once and for all the maladies caused by their stay on Earth.

One of their main arenas of study involved the differences between the plants on Rizq and the ones here on Earth. Within the vegetation filled botanical laboratories of Ebineru, the many formulas of life and death that they discovered were all recorded onto small Mae Stone crystals. Among the varieties of living creatures that they studied, Enki became especially enamored by the tall, slender hominids living in the tall trees who used their front legs as hands. Every so often, he would see them walking erect among the tall grasses. One of the things in particular that fascinated Enki was the creature's compassion for the other beings of the jungle. It would go about and actually *release* the animals they had been capturing from their traps.

Becoming so fully absorbed in these studies, Enki hadn't notice the problems in the mines until Commander Ennugi radioed him personally with news of the most recent developments in the Abzu.

"My lord, I cannot continue pushing my crews like this," Ennugi said. "Their complaints have gone unheeded and now, they are threatening to quit altogether," he told him with a tone in his voice that verged on insubordination. "A higher yield will be inconsequential if all production is shut down!"

"This is truly disturbing news, Commander," Enki said. "But, I can assure you that I have been concerned that this day would come for a long time. It is due to the depth of my current research that I have been inattentive to the conditions there. I'm pleased to inform you though, that our recent studies have discovered an alternative that may actually alleviate our people's toil in the Abzu…for good."

Enki told Ennugi of his plan to create the new worker. Then, without wanting to get the commander involved, he secretly coached the mining crew on how to trap Enlil in order to manipulate him into accepting the plan for the new worker that he had conceived. He knew that Enlil would oppose his idea for using the ape-man's design to create a substitute workforce. Initiating Enki's covert plan, the miners in the Abzu dramatically reduced their shipment of gold ore to Bad-Tibira.

Chapter Eight

It was Ninutra who had noticed the drop in ore being brought from the Abzu to Bad-Tibira for refinement, and he contacted the Head of Command immediately. Enlil was consumed in his duties when the young commander's holographic image appeared within the crystalline dome on his office desk in Nibru-ki.

"Hello, my son," he said without looking up from what he was doing.

"Father, we have a situation here in Bad-Tibira. It has recently been brought to my attention that the ore shipments from the Abzu have been drastically reduced for some inexplicable reason," he reported.

Enlil looked up from his computer and turned to Ninutra, now giving him his complete, undivided attention. "This *is* most unusual," he said, as he stroked his chin whiskers in concerned contemplation. "I want you to go down there," he said sternly. "Find out why this is happening and report back to me immediately."

Ninutra bowed his head. "As you wish, my lord."

✦ ✦ ✦

When Ninutra arrived at the Abzu, he met with Lord Enki, and Commander Ennugi escorted the two of them to the excavation site personally. Once there, Ninutra experienced firsthand the backbiting, grumbling and lament of the workers. They were quite displeased and complained that the work was unbearable and extremely unsafe.

"As you can see, Ninutra, these miners are under a tremendous amount of stress. It seems that all at once, many have reported to be too ill to work, and many have been requesting extensive amounts of time off for physical recovery," Enki explained. "Report what you've seen to Enlil. Tell him to come to the Abzu himself to see firsthand how these miners suffer."

Ninutra contacted Enlil and he agreed to make the trip down to the Abzu.

Upon his arrival, he was stationed in a small command center located just outside the excavation site's entrance, in a building that looked much like a giant, beige stucco pumpkin.

Cave-ins were not uncommon deep within the mines and Enki figured the next one would be all it would take to justify a rebellion ... it was just a matter of time. So when a major disaster did happen in one of the mine shafts, the miners were coached by Enki to unnerve Enlil and gain their relief through hostilities.

Finally, something *did* happen, and the call went out through the workforce. The miners' rioted on cue, setting fire to tools and equipment.

✦ ✦ ✦

Enki knew it would be bad, but not this bad ... when the crewman rushed into his laboratory, he was sitting at his workstation in front of a monitor, deep in thought.

"My lord ...! The mining crews are staging the rebellion but the extent of this new cave-in is beyond anything we had predicted."

Since the day they started mining the Abzu, the lives of these miners had changed dramatically. No longer were these people on their home world living mundane lives of farming or service to the elite, they were now clawing down through hundreds of miles of black earth, drilling into the heart of the Abzu, not knowing from one minute to the next if they would live to see the next day, let alone the next moment.

Only the elite had access to the regenerative sciences that made them virtually immortal. The life span of the lower classes stationed on Earth was only generally six to nine hundred years. Since the first day they started operations, several generations had worked the mines. Theirs was a life of risk, particularly from cave-ins, but to those willing, the financial rewards and prestige could be great. On their search within the earth for gold, one of the biggest issues the workers had faced was constantly having to wade through the slurry of runoff from the massive water cannons that were used in the pressure cutting of their large tunnels.

Now, all simple issues seemed quite trivial. The demands for a higher yield had created fewer safety protocols in the new corridors. The underlying truth of the matter, is that overworked miners were bound to make mistakes. The messenger had brought more news from the latest cave-in...and it was catastrophic. They'd had some cave-ins over the countless years that they'd been mining the Abzu but the rescue squads, specially trained over the centuries, had been successful nearly every time...until this time.

As Enki boarded the small tram that would take him to the site to inspect collapsed mineshaft QX-19743, he tensed, not knowing exactly what he would do when he got there. He thought of Enlil and surmised what his brother would be thinking of the bad news. Normally Enlil would have simply ordered the miners right back to work once the bodies were cleared out. Now he was going to be at the mercy of an angry mob. He might soon be thinking a little differently. Enki thought of Ninmah and knew that she would have heard the news by now. She must be very concerned about the men and what was happening here.

In no time, the shuttle transporting him from Ebineru had reached the massive hole that went into the earth. During the trip, Enki was briefed on the cave-in details and reassured that during the rebellion, Enlil was just going to be held by the miners and would not be harmed. As Enki disembarked, he was greeted by a crewman who accompanied him to the next tram that would take him deeper into the mines.

As they got closer, a thick, hazy cloud came toward them...
it was dust from the cave-in. Enki's eyes became gritty and he
coughed. The tram pressed onward.

As they reached the edge of a high cliff, down below, Enki could
see the bodies of the workers that had been killed piled in a heap
in an open area outside of the mouth of the massive corridor.
Slowly, more of the bodies that had been broken by heavy rock
and smothered by toxic fumes were added to the pile of casualties.

Ennugi and Ninutra were busy directing the rescue crews when
they saw Enki arrive. As soon as they had finished their instructions to the teams, they hurried over to speak with him.

"My lord, we have a *very* high body count this time," Ennugi
said. "The miners are furious... equipment has been vandalized...
they have had enough." He averted his eyes, sure that such
confrontational demeanor could potentially lead to punishment
for insubordination. But Enki could tell that Ennugi did not care
about himself at that point and that his main concern was for the
miners. He respected that.

Enki moved toward the highest point of the cliff. One of the
attendants tried to keep him back, concerned that he was too close
to the edge, but he just shrugged him off. Even though he had been
coaching the mining crews in rebellion and a catastrophe such as
this was inevitable, the workers now needed to hear from him
directly. Upon sight of Lord Enki, the scattered miners slowly
hobbled together into a cluster below him. Against the background
of the smoldering, burned-out digging machines, the hardships of
a lifetime of mining showed on the many weary reptilian faces.
They were haggard, dirty... and *very* angry. Enki raised his arms
and the rabble of angry hissing slowly ceased.

"Upon reviewing the details of today's cave-in," Enki began, "I
am in agreement with you all, and I must put an end to this." He
lowered his arms, looked down and shook his head. He was
empathetic with their plight. Looking back up slowly, he gazed out
over the assembled crowd.

"Demands for a higher yield...and a lax in safety protocols have caused this catastrophe." He paused, "Being continuously exposed to this harsh environment...working these dangerous mines for generation upon generation...it is absolutely appalling!"

The miners all agreed as they looked at one another and raised their arms while they shouted.

"YYAAAAAHHHHHH...!"

"I have seen the Galaxy," Enki continued, "and there is so much more out there." He scanned the crowd. "I do not blame you for wanting to lay down your tools and revolt." He looked down for a moment, then back up to address the crowd. He was *not* going to allow this atrocity to continue.

Enki raised his fist and shouted, "My loyalty and understanding goes out to you all."

Members of the crowd grumbled and shook their heads in disbelief, and he couldn't blame them. They didn't know him. All they knew was that the ruling class was safe and protected in their ships and palaces, with no day-to-day worries like the miners had. He raised his hands again to quiet them.

"Though the mining must continue...we *will* find another way!"

The crowd broke into a loud cheer.

"RAAAAAHHHHH...!"

Soon after word of Enki's speech on the cliff reached Enlil, he went immediately to where Enki was. When he got to the site, he seemed a little shaken but more outraged than anything.

"Enki, what have you done! You cannot simply offer these men empty promises. It will only incite them to more dissension when we cannot deliver!" he growled angrily.

"No need to worry, brother," Enki said coolly. "There's been a severe lack of understanding between us and them. They need to know just what they are giving their lives for and that this is still a noble cause. They feel that we don't care."

He turned to face Enlil. "But we do care...at least I do. They need to know that they can count on us. I assure you, we will find a solution to all of this."

"Don't be too sure about that," Enlil snarled. "You've succeeded in calming them down for now, but what about the next time? What happens when there is another disaster such as this one?"

"There won't be a next time." Enki said, with certainty. *I'm going to make sure of that,* he thought to himself.

The extent of Enki's plan was put into full swing that night when a group of miners cornered Ennugi in a remote mine shaft. Seizing him, he was taken by force to the command post where Enlil was stationed. Holding him at the gates, the group surrounded the small building, torches and tools held high as they yelled and shouted angrily.

The guard at the gate summoned Nusku—Enlil's vizier—to tell him of what was happening, and he hurried to Enlil's chambers to wake him from his sleep.

"My lord...! The building is surrounded by an armed group of angry workers," he said in a hushed tone.

Enlil got up immediately, and he was furious. "So it's mutiny is it? Alert Enki, and I will confront these rebels myself."

Nusku summoned Enki, who sent Ninutra to see to the situation. Meanwhile, from a balcony above the building's entranceway, Enlil confronted the angry mob.

"So...! Who among you speaks for this unruly group of conspirators amassed before me?

The crowd reacted in unison as they shouted out. One worker spoke from within the assembled mass and yelled up to him, "We are united my lord! Together we stand...as a group we are one!"

Another angry miner spoke out. "The work here is excessive, heavy and quite distressful, my lord! We have had enough!"

Enlil stared out over the large crowd of angry miners who had his residence surrounded. He was fuming with the rage of a captured animal. *How dare these men threaten the High Commander and heir to the throne!* he thought to himself. Livid, he turned away from the crowd to contact his father on the home world.

Anu's image was already present within the crystal on Enlil's desk when he got back to his chambers.

"Father...! I am being held captive by a mob of workers," he snarled, drool dripping from the corners of his mouth. "You must help me deal with this rebellion!"

"My son...be calm. I am aware of your plight." Anu said sternly. Enki's holographic image now came up within the crystalline dome with Anu.

"Enki, of what is Enlil being accused?"

"My lord, the miners are angry about the working conditions, not Enlil," Enki responded. "The outcry of their suffering is heavy and complaints are filed on a daily basis. I have tried to assure them that relief will come, but at this point it doesn't seem to be enough."

"That may be the case, and I sympathize with our Anunaki workforce, but the mining must continue because this gold *must* be obtained," Lord Anu said calmly. "Enki, I want you to go there and speak with the miners. Tell them to release Ennugi and we will consult with *him* on this matter."

When Enki arrived at the scene, Ninutra was already inside the building with his father. He spoke with the miners and had Ennugi released, and the two of them went inside to have their meeting with Lord Anu. Once inside Enlil's chambers, they contacted the king once again and his holographic image reappeared within the crystal dome. Anu immediately turned to Ennugi and addressed him directly, "Ennugi, you are closer than anyone to what is happening down there—assess the situation for me."

Unlike Enki and Enlil, Ennugi stood at attention, as he was not accustomed to being in the presence of his Majesty the king.

"My lord...aside from the usual hardships, lately the heat and dangerous gas levels have been rising significantly, making work even more unbearable than ever." Ennugi broke his ridged stance and addressed Anu less candidly. "What is needed the most, my lord, is a complete renovation of systems, tools and equipment."

Ninutra interjected, "Why not simply send the rebels back to Rizq and replace them with a new mining crew? With better equipment and a fresh crew, we should have production levels back and maintain a higher efficiency rate in the process."

Enlil broke in. "I agree that our extraction methods are outdated." He turned to Enki, "Can you design new tools...so that tunnel work can be completely automated?" Narrowing his eyes and stroking his chin whiskers, Enki thought it *might* be possible as he nodded to the affirmative.

"As for the rebels," Enlil continued, "they should be tried for *treason*, not sent home! How dare they threaten the Lord of the Command?" Enki glanced at him briefly, knowing the actual truth of the matter, but he held his tongue for the moment.

"We will deal with the issue of the rebels in due time," Anu told them. "Until then, we will make arrangements to proceed with replacing them and redesigning our operations." The transmission ended and the king's image faded from within the crystalline monitor.

When Enlil returned to Nibru-ki, the first thing he did was go to his office and contact his father for a more private discussion about the situation at hand. On his desk, the holographic image of Lord Anu appeared. Enki's image from Ebineru was also within the monitor in its lower corner and they were already in the middle of a conversation. Enlil interrupted them, still furious about the recent course of events.

"This is outrageous, Father!" Enlil shouted as he paced in front of the domed crystal monitor. "The continued success of this mission *depends* on the mining of the gold we're getting from these operations! We can't just shut down production!" he said, as he balled his hand into a fist and slammed it on the computer console.

"When I asked them who had instigated the rebellion, they told me they were standing together as a group, but in truth, it was *Enki* who had originally aroused them!" he said, pointing a clawed finger at his brother. He promised them relief that we simply can't provide." He continued, "Yes, I'm well aware that they complain the work is excessive, heavy and distressful, and I am well aware that these are long standing issues. But these miners, as far as I'm concerned, are mutineers!"

Sitting at his desk in his misty, plant-filled Ebineru office, Enki remained silent throughout the whole of Enlil's outburst.

"These men are criminals," Enlil shouted, "and they need to be brought into custody, tried and punished to the maximum degree of the law...as an example!" He leaned into the monitor and snarled, drool dripping from the corners of his angry mouth.

"Father, we *must* retain control in this matter! We may not even need them! We could easily design new equipment...equipment that will make the tunnel work automated."

"My brother...you must relax," Enki said, calmly. "Realistically, we cannot *completely* automate our systems, and I don't plan on simply replacing the teams with more Anunaki from the home world. These miners have mutinied under my encouragement and my support."

Enlil was completely stunned, and became enraged when he heard Enki finally admit what he had done.

"What—?" he bellowed. "Your support!"

"Yes." Enki said adamantly. "You see, expecting our brothers to toil endlessly here on Earth is no longer a viable option." He paused, as he let the reality of his statement fully sink in. "When I look at my Rizqian brothers doing this menial labor, I think of all *we've* seen. The bulk of our mining crews are descendants of the six hundred crew members we had originally employed and the others were never told of how strenuous this environment would be. For most, all they have *known* is a harsh life of mining here on Earth."

Enki's demeanor was tranquil, but Enlil was fuming as he looked at his father for some kind of supportive response. His face was unreadable. Enki continued.

"Think about it... These are people, not merely components of industry. Don't they *deserve* the opportunity to live normal lives?"

Enki reached for a nearby control panel with an assortment of Mae Stones set into it. He removed one of the blue crystals and inserted it into the computer console in front of him. The holographic image of the hominid that Enki had been studying now rotated in the corner of Enlil's monitor.

At that moment, Ninmah, Ninutra and Enki's son Ningishzida, unexpectedly entered the Nibru-ki control room. When Enlil noticed them, he composed himself immediately, not wanting to show weakness in their presence. Enki had summoned them from Shurubak, Ebineru and Bad-Tibira to be part of what he was about to propose.

"Within your monitors is a being that exists within the jungles of the Abzu," Enki said, as the monkey-man image became larger from the corner of the crystalline monitor. "Its genetics will be the foundation of a new workforce that we will design specifically for our needs within the Earth environment," he explained.

The commanders were completely speechless. Ninmah stood there and gently shook her elegantly horned head, perplexed.

Realistically—she didn't feel that it could be done.

"This is all very good hypothetically... but these beings don't exist," Enlil said impatiently. "I've never seen, or even heard of them."

"These creatures *do* exist, deep within the jungles of the Abzu, and I am certain that they are just what we need." Enki brought up some prerecorded clips of the creature eating with its hands and walking upright on its hind legs in the jungle and on the sierra plains. "I call the hominoid monkey-man—Australopithecus."

The commanders were astounded as Enki showed them the footage of the rare and unique creature.

"Ningishzida and I have been developing a template for an efficient and effective design that will leave the mark of our essence on this being," Enki said. Ninmah pondered to herself upon how their own ancestors may have possibly looked like these creatures ... animals that were more like beings than creatures.

Within Enlil's monitor, the holographic image of the indigenous mammal came up into the center of the crystal dome overlaying their father's, as his reduced to the bottom of the screen. Next to the Australopithecus, an image of an average Rizqian worker appeared, and then ... the holographic images of the two types of men blended. Enlil tensed at the very thought of a genetically modified Earth creature. In his mind, this was *not* an option to be explored.

The new image showed a creature that was a somewhat smaller version of the Anunaki but with minor hominoid traits. Standing seven feet tall and covered in small green scales, it had a soft beige underbelly, but no horns or tail. The being had a rather large, round head that was set with big, dark, round eyes, small nose slits and an expressionless slit of a mouth.

"Within your monitors is a prototype of a being we have been exploring for the creation of a primitive workforce. We plan to crossbreed our genetics with one of the most evolved species here on Earth, this highly intelligent hominid, the Australopithecus. It can be genetically designed specifically to fit our needs for our operations in the Abzu," he explained.

"The newly designed creature will carry our dominant saurian features, and characteristics—yet their underlying mammalian physiology will make them highly adaptable to the inner Earth environments. Our plan is to create a *warm-blooded* reptilian being devoid of the undesirable physical traits of mammalian beings. Our cold-blooded, reptilian physiology has always required a regulated, external environment and with these creatures, this issue would be eliminated. Because of its internal, mammalian thermostat ... this creature will be capable of adapting to a variety of climatic variations," he concluded.

The presentation had successfully managed to gain Lord Anu's interest, who was now stroking his chin whiskers and nodding his head from within the monitor.

"Enlil, I want you and your commanders to go to the Abzu," he told them. "Enki can give us a complete tour of his labs and we will see this Australopithecus he speaks of for ourselves."

✦ ✦ ✦

Upon the commanders arrival at Ebineru, Enki took the group to his outdoor laboratory and showed them to the holding areas, where he had some of the monkey-man creatures captive in barred, metal cages. At the sight of Enki and the others, the beasts began jumping up and down, beating on the cage bars with their fists angrily grunting, snorting and howling.

When they had completed their inspection, the group left the pens where the animals were being held and they returned to the clean, white laboratories inside Enki's complex. From within a crystal dome set on top of a large computer console, Lord Anu watched from the home world as Enki explained his plans to the commanders.

"These creatures have male and female genitalia and procreate in a similar fashion to the way we do," Enki told them. "We have tested their DNA, and it is remarkably quite similar to our own."

"Once complete, the being will be reptilian in its overall appearance and thoroughly capable of handling tools designed for excavation labor."

It was obvious that Enlil was repulsed by Enki's presentation, and he spoke up immediately, quoting an ancient Universal Prime Directive.

"My lords...this plan is an atrocity! For one thing, it is well known by *all* beings capable of interplanetary star travel, that the interfering with and altering of indigenous life forms on other worlds is highly forbidden.

"We came to this world to obtain gold...*not* to play—God!"

"And besides...our people abolished this kind of slavery *eons* ago," he continued. "We now have machines that do our work for us!"

Enki responded calmly and said simply, "Think of these beings as helpers...not slaves."

Ninmah had been quiet throughout the presentation and she finally gave her opinion. "Considering that these beings *do* already exist...by altering them, we would only be making them better. Yes...it may be a bit unorthodox, but I say that if we have the will and Destiny has given us the technology to accomplish the task, why *shouldn't* we use it?" she asked.

Ninutra felt that his father was right. "With all that we have accomplished technologically, instead of creating this race of slave beings—we must surely have the capacity to create the new tools we'll need to counteract our obstacles."

Ningishzida turned to him and explained, "With what we already know about these Earth beings, a destined, natural course of events would lead us to create these new worker beings eventually. With the scientific knowledge we now posses...its ultimate use simply cannot be prevented."

"Well, this is truly the real question, isn't it?" Enki posed. "Is it a matter of Destiny—from the beginning ordained, or is it Fate—by us, for the choosing?"

✦ ✦ ✦

On Rizq, Lord Anu presented the issue before the High Council, who pondered heavily on the matter. They spoke to one another of Life and Death... and of Destiny and Fate; but ultimately—survival won the argument and the Rules of Interplanetary Travel were ultimately forsaken. They would create the worker being, and the safety of their home world of Rizq would be ensured.

The commanders from Edin returned to their posts, as everyone waited for a response from the home world. In Nibru-ki, Anu's holographic image suddenly filled the largest crystal monitor of its main control room. He wasted no time with formalities. "The new workforce that Enki has been designing sounds very promising," he said. "We will allow the dismissal of the miners in time...and authorize the creation of replacement workers." He gave a stern look. "I expect to be informed of your results in detail as they progress." The king's image left the large crystal dome as the transmission terminated abruptly. With Ninmah by his side, Enlil sat silently in front of the monitor as he processed the council's decision.

Enki's image now filled the large screen and he was delighted. As he spoke to Enlil, his gaze toward his sister suggested a longing he did very little to conceal. "Brother, may I request...that because of her great understanding of these matters, Ninmah assist us in the creation of this new being down here in the Abzu?"

Enlil exhaled with a humph and just shook his head at the whole turn of events. He looked over at Ninmah, and she bowed her head respectfully. "As you wish," he said flatly, having completely given up on argument at this point.

Back in the Abzu, Ennugi informed the mining teams that until the new worker was created, they would have to willingly go back to work. With the rebellion squelched, the disappointed Anunaki crew went back to their jobs while they waited for the new Primitive Worker to be created.

Chapter Nine

Enki, Ninmah and Ningishzida were now able to proceed with the plans for the new life form with the consent of the official proclamation of Lord Anu and the blessings of the High Council. At this point, Enki had not seen much of Enlil, whom he knew was still fuming about their father's siding with genetic manipulation; it was a satisfying feeling, however brief.

In Enki's Ebineru office, a thin mist gently covered the floor of the dimly lit, plant-filled room. Seated in a chair that looked as if it used to be some kind of enormous, alien insect at one time, Ninmah and Ningishzida stood at Enki's side. They were working in front of an illuminated computer console made of many different multicolored crystal panels, positioned next to view monitors with a variety of schematics within them. Enki and Ningishzida were busy explaining to Ninmah in great detail about their research and how they would be creating their new worker.

When they were finished, Enki took Ninmah outside to a place among some trees that was full of a number of random cages. There, within the cages, were the odd creatures from his experiments that he had chosen *not* to show the commanders earlier. He and Ningishzida had been creating them by splicing their genetic codes. Some of these beings had the foreparts of one kind of animal and the hind parts of another.

Returning to the House of Life, Enki showed Ninmah to the clean, brightly lit laboratories where they had been doing their experiments. She looked at the strange beings in their glass cages with intrigue, but overall, she was appalled at their plight.

"Enki...! These creatures are an abomination," she exclaimed. "And one can only imagine their suffering. They really should be destroyed, my lord!"

Enki looked calmly at the genetically spliced animals in their glass cages and said, "I agree with you. That is why you're here, my dear sister." He turned to her and gently placed his hand on her shoulder. "We need your expertise so that we will know how much essence to combine within our mixture. We need to know which womb the conception should be made in, and which womb should be used for birthing?"

Enki looked into her eyes. "We need the expertise and understanding of one who has actually given birth," he said, with a tone of deep respect. Ninmah smiled softly as she thought about their two beautiful daughters.

Ninmah studied the Mae Stones Sacred Life formulas with Ningishzida and he explained to her how he had manipulated the particular genetic combinations of the creatures that they had already created. Now, it was time to examine the Australopithecus creature's physiology and genetic coding more closely.

"The two-legged monkey creatures are fascinating...and they are actually quite similar to us in many ways," Ninmah said to him softly. "Have the two of you considered having an Anunaki male impregnate an Australopithecus female through the act of *sexual* intercourse?"

Enki looked up from his workstation. The question was unusual but completely valid. "Yes, well...we have tried that, and the results have always ended in a failed conception within the female," he explained.

Enki's team had finally come to the conclusion that the new being would have to be created in a series of stages, adding small Anunaki elements as they went. From the formulas on the Mae

Stones, they carefully calculated the Siriun elements that would be added to their creations. With their computers and the data collected on Mae Stones, they used high-tech medical equipment from their home world to perform the delicate procedures. Dressed in full surgical hood, mask and gloves, Ninmah artificially inseminated a female Australopithecus egg with an Anunaki sperm, in a small, quartz Petri dish.

The small vessel containing the inseminated egg was placed inside the womb of the Australopithecus female, and this time they had successful conception. A birth was now forthcoming.

✦ ✦ ✦

The team waited the allotted time for the baby's birth but the infant remained within the womb. In desperation, Ninmah made a cut and pulled the baby out with tongs. They were all quite relieved when they saw that the creature was alive and breathing.

Enki cried out, "We have done it!" and Ningishzida beamed proudly. Ninmah held the newborn in her hands, and she was not as pleased. The newborn was completely covered with shaggy hair, its upper body being very similar to that of the ape creatures. Only its legs and feet exhibited any kind of actual Anunaki traits.

"We should let the two-legged female nurse the newborn with her own milk," Ninmah said, and they gave the baby to its birth mother to suckle.

The being grew fast, but as the child grew taller, it did not resemble the being they had envisioned. Its hands were not suited for tools and its speech was only grunting sounds.

When the team had a meeting to discuss the project, Ninmah was direct. "This creature is in no way suited to our purposes. We must try again," she told them, and they both agreed.

Working directly with the information recorded in the Mae Stones, she adjusted the genome within the Anunaki seed, and with Enki and Ningishzida's help, they repeated the procedure. Ninmah studied the Maes very carefully as she took the genetic components and combined them in their precise sequence. With great skill, she then inseminated another female Australopithecus egg and inserted it in the female beast. After a time, it gave birth and to their delight, this time the child had much more of an Anunaki likeness.

The mother suckled the newborn and the team let it grow to be a young child. They found its looks to be appealing and its hands were good for grasping tools, but when they tested his senses, they found them to be deficient. His vision was poor and he could not hear. Working with the Mae Stone formulas, Ninmah rearranged and experimented with the genetic admixtures time, and time again, to ultimately create a proper design.

One of the beings had paralyzed feet, while another's semen was dripping. One had trembling hands and another had a malfunctioning liver. One's arms were too short to reach its mouth and one had lungs unsuitable for breathing. At this point, Enki was starting to get impatient and a little discouraged.

"With all that we have attempted, we *still* haven't produced a Primitive Worker," he grumbled. "Maybe we should shut down the program and pursue...something else!"

Ninmah was too absorbed in her studies of a small duckbilled mammal they had recently discovered on a remote Earth continent to empathize with his frustration. "I am discovering what is good and bad within our being by a series of trial and error." She stopped the genetic analysis she was doing and looked over at him. "In my heart, I know that if I pursue my current path, it *will* lead to a successful outcome. Be patient, my lord, we will find our sequence."

Once more, a formula was composed, and once more, the new born was deficient. Upon further examination of all they had done, Enki discovered something that he thought might possibly be significant. "Perhaps the shortfall is not in the admixture or the womb, but in that their vessels of insemination are made of an element foreign to this world—quartz crystal from Rizq. Let's try making these specimen dishes out of an Earth clay instead."

Ninmah was impressed. "You may have something there, my dear... A quite brilliant deduction actually. Yes—why hadn't I thought of it before?"

"There is a clay near the mines that is rich in minerals," Enki added. "The trace elements of copper and iron may be the exact component needed to perfect our equation." He was pleased that they had finally made some kind of a breakthrough, even if it was only hypothetical. "I will arrange to have some delivered to us immediately," he told her.

When it arrived, Ninmah fashioned small vessels out of the Abzu clay. After they had all been fired and sterilized, she gently placed an Australopithecus egg and an Anunaki sperm in one of them.

Upon consulting the formulas on her computer's Mae Stones, she added the appropriate genome sequences, and the delicate process was completed as she placed the fertilized egg within the female host.

Ninmah had been patiently monitoring the mammal's progress from her workstation when she announced proudly, "We have done it, my lords! There is conception within the female beast."

Enki and Ningishzida were both very relieved to hear the news.

When the allotted time for the pregnancy had passed, the female Australopithecus went into labor and, with the group's assistance; she gave birth to a male child. Holding the infant in her hands, Ninmah examined its form. It was a vision of perfection. The child looked reptilian, with no mutations. Her team was ecstatic.

"This is a wonderful achievement, Sister!" Enki said, as he slapped Ningishzida on the back joyfully. He embraced Ninmah and kissed her. "You have done it...! You have created our Worker being!" he said to her with a gleam in his eye. When they gave the newborn to its mother to suckle, they took a moment as they discussed what the creature might actually look like when it was fully developed.

The child grew up quickly and although the being had limbs

suited for working, he was incapable of speaking words, only grunts and snorts.

"We are very close to having our Worker being," Enki announced to his team. "We must consider all the steps that have been taken so far," he glanced over at his sister, "During the process, there *was* one thing we never changed...we have always used the Earth mammal's wombs for our conceptions."

Ninmah looked at him, bewildered. "What are you saying?"

"Perhaps it is an Anunaki womb that is required to *truly* create a worker in our likeness." There was silence in the laboratory. Until now, the idea had been unheard of and never really considered. They all stared silently at each other, wondering what the other was thinking.

After some consideration, Ninmah agreed that Enki's point was indeed valid. "Perhaps the admixture *is* in the wrong womb, but what Anunaki female would offer her womb freely to this kind of experiment? What if the child they would be carrying turns out to be some kind of hideous monster?" Ninmah asked him with a slight tremble in her voice.

"I could ask my wife Ninki to carry the child," Enki said. "I will summon her to Ebineru and we can present our plan to her." He reached over to touch the panel that would make the call and Ninmah put her hand on his shoulder.

"No! No! These formulas are my design. The rewards and the dangers should be mine alone. I will provide the womb and accept fate, whatever the outcome."

Enki bowed his head. "So be it," he said softly.

Working together, they created the new admixture of Rizqian sperm and introduced it to the Australopithecus egg. When it was ready, Enki gently placed the fertilized egg inside of Ninmah, and a successful conception *was* achieved, but no one knew how long the pregnancy would actually last. In the end, it did take longer than the usual nine months for maturation and there were some legitimate concerns raised. Everything was fine though, and in time

Ninmah gave birth to a healthy male child. As Enki held the infant in his hands, he found it to be an image of perfection, and when he slapped it on the rear end, he was quite satisfied to hear that it made the proper sounds that they were hoping for.

He handed Ninmah the child and she held it up, "We have done it!" she cried out. When she held the baby to her breast to suckle, she felt a well-deserved sense of pride in her accomplishment.

As Ningishzida examined the child, he was quite pleased with their most recent creation as well. "It appears...that we have attained perfection at last," he said with confident elation.

The child had a soft-scaled skin like the Anunaki, and when Enki saw Ninmah with the child, he saw them as a mother and a son, not a mother and a creature. "What will you call this being?" he asked her.

Ninmah touched the child's face gently. "Lulu," she told him softly.

Enki walked over to where Ningishzida was working. "Now Son, I would like to know more about this being's design." Within the crystal dome in front of them, the holographic image of the adult Lulu changed. The new worker being stopped its rotation and was now overlaid with technical logistics.

"As you can see, the Lulu has our dominant reptilian traits. However, the mammalian elements we have added will make it highly adaptive to harsh mining environments," he explained. "Their warm-blooded componenentry has been designed to allow them to adapt to surroundings within the range of sixty degrees Fahrenheit."

An image of its eyeball appeared with a large, dilated iris. "I have also altered their optic nerve," Ningishzida said, "to enable them better vision within dark environments."

"It seems that we now have a prime model for our Primitive Worker," said Enki with a renewed sense of confidence in all the work they had done.

"Father...a host of workers will be required to fill our needs in the Abzu," Ningishzida reminded him.

"Yes, I am aware of that," said Enki. "This original Lulu shall be given special treatment and protected from work to ensure that our mold for the others is preserved." Ninmah looked down softly at the newborn infant she held in her arms when she overheard this and was very pleased.

"Now...whose wombs shall carry the fertilized eggs for our work-force?" Enki said, as he looked over at his sister and stroked his chin whiskers contemplatively.

"I will ask my team of female doctors in Shurubak if any of them would be willing to volunteer," said Ninmah.

With Enlil's approval, she summoned her team to the House of Life and within the nursery of the laboratories, she showed them the newborn Earthling. "The task of surrogacy is by no means a command; it is to be offered by free will alone," she told them. Out of the group of female doctors, seven of them were willing to take the risk and they stepped forward to accept the task.

Their names were recorded onto stone tablets and the women were praised as heroes. As Ninmah prepared the seven clay vessels for the surrogates, she said an incantation over them to ensure their success.

"Within this genetic mixture, Earthling and Anunaki shall be bound. In unity, two essences...one of Heaven, one of Earth...shall be brought together as one."

Ningishzida recorded her words and her process, and the small ceramic vessels were placed inside the wombs of the volunteer surrogates. With the skill of their medical precision, insemination was successfully achieved within them all, and the team awaited their successful conceptions.

When the time came nine months later, the women successfully give birth to seven healthy male infants. To everyone's delight, their features were aesthetically correct and they made proper sounds. That evening, Ninmah quietly monitored the newborns as they suckled their mothers in bays that lined the circular walls of her softly lit Ebineru laboratory.

Ningishzida was excited with the scope of their current progress and he looked over at his father, "We have created seven Workers, my lord. Now... let's make seven more!"

Enki shook his head, "My son... not even seven times seven would be sufficient. The task would be too much to ask of these surrogates; they would be pregnant for an eternity." he told him.

Ninmah agreed. "The task would be much too demanding and slow beyond reason," she said in a hushed voice as she looked over at the medical bays.

"Well then, I suppose we should start the process of creating a female counter part to our Lulu, so that it will procreate and create more Primitive Workers," Ningishzida told them.

"Yes... we can adjust the formula within the Mae Stone and switch the male genome to a female one," said Enki. "We will need another Anunaki surrogate to host the child though."

Enki looked at Ninmah and before she could speak, he raised his hand. "Let me summon my wife Ninki this time," he said with a strong voice. "If she is willing, she will be the one to carry the female Lulu."

They summoned Ninki to Ebineru and laid out their plans to her. The team told her of what would be required of her and of the potential dangers. Ninki explained to them how she found the whole experiment to be quite fascinating actually and she agreed to go through with the procedure quite willingly.

Ningishzida adjusted the formulas within their Mae Stone and inseminated the mammalian egg with the new admixture. He then placed the fertilized egg within the womb of Ninki, and as in the surrogates before, there was a successful conception. After they had waited the allotted time for the pregnancy, the baby was not forthcoming, and after the tenth month, they were beginning to become concerned for Ninki and the child.

In the lab, Ninmah suited up for the operation. She made an incision above Ninki's vagina with skilled precision and performed a cesarean birth. As Ninmah removed the child, her face lit up when she saw the healthy newborn Lulu infant. After the delivery, they examined the baby closely and discovered that she was properly proportioned and had no defects. When they spanked her bottom, to their delight, she cried out proper sounds. They gave the newborn back to Ninki to suckle and nourish, and they allowed her to raise it to maturity. It was from this female that the other Lulu females would soon be created.

When the time came, Ninmah prepared the vessels made of Abzu clay and readied them for insertion into her seven volunteer surrogates. Once again, all women conceived successfully, and in time they bore seven perfect female Lulu children. The team was very pleased to find all of their features to be proper and their words to be sound.

While Enki examined the children's charts closely, Ninmah and Ningishzida waited in anticipation of his conclusions.

"These creatures are perfectly healthy," he told them. "When they have grown to maturity they will begin to procreate and we will then have a vast workforce at our disposal. The Lulu will soon bear the toil of the Anunaki."

The team was extremely pleased with the level of their current achievement, so they all took a moment to drink special elixir to celebrate their success.

✦ ✦ ✦

Large cages were made for the Lulu children and placed in the trees, where the males and females were allowed to grow up together. It was expected that, in time, the males would eventually mate with and impregnate the females.

Enki and his team took the two original Lulu from the Abzu to

Eridu, where they were put into a special enclosure and allowed to roam freely. Anunaki elite and crewmembers from every outpost came to see the new beings that Enki and his team had created.

Since the day they had started, Enlil had never been pleased with the experiment, but that displeasure quickly diminished when he gazed upon the young Lulu.

Ninutra came to see the new prototypes and so did Ninlil. From the way station on Mars, Marduk came, and so did the Igigi who shuttled gold. They all came to see the new creatures, and they were completely in awe.

The consensus was mutual. "You have done it," they all would tell them. "You have created a Primitive Worker . . . our days of toil on Earth have ended!"

Pleased with the results of their presentation, Enki, Ninmah and Ningishzida left Eridu and returned to the House of Life, down in the Abzu. There, the newborns were getting bigger and the Enki's team anticipated their soon coming to maturity.

Deep in the mining pit of the Abzu, the Anunaki were still grumbling as they became impatient for their relief. Ennugi often inquired on the progress made on the Primitive Worker and conveyed the outcry for their highly anticipated application. The time for the Lulu's maturity was now overdue and there was still no noticeable conception observed among the females.

Ningishzida decided to make himself a couch out of grass to put up in the trees so he could sit and watch the Lulu interact within their cages. He watched what they did throughout the day and night and found that the Lulu were indeed mating. The females were being inseminated, but they were not conceiving.

When Enki was told of this, he pondered the matter deeply as he recalled all the many creatures they had combined. Among them, none . . . not one of them, had been capable of producing offspring. He looked at his son despairingly. "Maybe we have created accursed creatures when we decided to start manipulating these genetic sequences," he said, with an abandoned sense of hope in all that they had done.

"Upon further examination of the Lulu DNA, my lords, it is now quite apparent that these beings sequencing lack two essential strands that govern the procreation process," Ningishzida explained. When Ninmah heard this, she was quite distraught and Enki was seized with horrible frustration, as he slammed his fist on his console surface.

"The clamor in the Abzu has been growing daily and another mutiny is surely in the making," he told them forcefully. "A Primitive Worker *must* be created soon, or else our gold extraction efforts will most certainly be shut down indefinitely." He shook his head as he looked at the floor. "We already have a being perfected…we will simply have to impregnate Anunaki surrogates in massive campaigns, no matter how tedious and impractical it may seem." He looked at Ninmah. "They will have to be brought here from Rizq, pending father's approval."

Enki stroked his chin whiskers as he weighed the depth of the decision. Ultimately, the success of their mission on Earth would take precedence in any decision made.

"Pay the volunteers whatever they need…just do what it takes to create this new workforce!"

In time, the host of one hundred surrogates from Rizq arrived at Baalbek. They were quickly transported to Ninmah's medical center of Shurubak, where they were made comfortable and then prepared for their artificially inseminated pregnancies.

From his misty, plant-filled office in Ebineru, Enki contacted his sister. Within his central monitor, the holographic image of her horned, birdlike face faded into view. She was in her medical laboratory in Shurubak. In the background, the multicolored crystal panels and buttons of her lab flashed repetitiously with a deep, soft droning hum. Enki looked up from his work to address her.

"Ninmah my dear, how is our Primitive Workforce project coming along?"

Ninmah turned in her chair to look at the dimly lit medical bays lining the curved walls within the large laboratory that housed the rows and rows of impregnated female Anunaki surrogates on reclined beds.

"Well my brother, we *have* had a few failures. But for the most part, we've had many successful gestations."

"Please elaborate," Enki said.

"At this point, all of our surrogates have been successfully impregnated with the Lulu being." The console screen split to show the holographic images of all the Lulu embryo gestating inside the surrogate wombs. A rotating image of a fully developed adult Lulu rotated next to them. The adult being looked much like the creature that they had originally designed, with its round head, big eyes and green reptilian skin.

"My team and I will be monitoring the volunteers on a regular basis," Ninmah said, as she looked over at the women lying in their medical bays.

When he had inspected all of Ninmah's diagrams, Enki nodded his approval. He put his hand to up the holographic image of Ninmah within the domed crystal monitor. "Sister...you have done well. We will inform the commanders of our results and await Father's final approval." He reached over and touched a blue crystal panel on his console to save all of their research onto one file. "When the order goes through...the workforce will be transported to the Abzu and soon the hardships within the mining operations will be relieved."

He paused for a moment as he gazed upon his sister's image. "My confidence in your abilities was well placed, Ninmah...We've done it."

Ninmah softly closed her eyes and bowed her head. Her hologram faded from the large crystal dome, but Enki continued to stare at it a while longer.

The one hundred recruited surrogates were systematically impregnated three times, carrying three male Lulu babies apiece.

When they had completed their gestations, the Anunaki had
created three hundred Lulu Workers. No longer needed, the surrogates were sent back to Rizq and the Lulu children were raised to
maturity in Shurubak.

The young Lulus were trained in the skills of mining and the
handling of equipment used in the mining processes. When they
had all fully matured, the workers looked just as Enki and his team
had originally envisioned. Standing seven feet tall, the creatures
were covered with dark green scales and had large, dark round eyes.
The time had now come to send them via shuttlecraft down to the
Abzu to do the jobs that they had been designed for.

Parked in rows on the large, sandstone spaceport plaza, a fleet of
small transport ships awaited the new mining force. Slowly, a large
group of Lulu line up in rows on the plaza and proceed to board
the small white ships. When they had all had been loaded, the fleet
of shuttlecrafts lift off one by one from the plaza at Shurubak and
head south to the mines of the African Abzu.

The Lulu workers understood the commands of the Anunaki
well and they were always eager to be with them, toiling well for
nothing more than food rations. They never complained about the
heat, dust or mud, and backbreaking work never seemed to bother
them.

At long last, the Anunaki were relieved from the hardships of
the Abzu and the overworked mining teams were finally allowed to
return home.

Chapter Ten

One hundred years on Earth went by, as the Lulu work-force gathered gold effectively and efficiently. They kept the machines running almost twenty-four hours a day. They were diligent creatures, almost tireless...up to a point.

Far underground, in a side tunnel of a larger mine shaft, a Lulu worker, haggard from age and labor, dug weakly at a vein of ore on a tunnel wall with a small handpick. It paused for a moment, then suddenly it shut down where it stood, falling over to take its final breaths on the tunnel floor. An Anunaki guard walked over to find the dead worker and gave a frustrated grunt. He walked over to an electronic panel imbedded in a nearby tunnel wall and pressed a small purple crystal panel.

"Sir, we have lost another Lulu in Quadrant c7-8...requesting a replacement drone at 12:38 hours."

A pause, then, "Request noted," said Operations. "Replacement to arrive in approximately forty-one days."

"Sir," the large reptilian guard said, displeased. "I have quotas to be met. Forty-one days is *unacceptable*!"

"Stand down, Lieutenant!" Operations said. "We have a large number of replacements to fill...accommodating the immediate demands will be a time-consuming process."

There was another pause as the guard waited. The Operations commander came back on the line, coldly and unsympathetically.

"Your request will be processed and your replacement will arrive as soon as it is ready."

"Thank you, sir," the guard said, with an obvious discontent. "I understand...be assured though, I *will* be filing a formal complaint with the Head of Command. Out!"

Within the Palace of Eridu, Enki sat in his mist filled office before a multicolored crystal console, in one of its dark, strangely shaped spiked chairs. He was consumed in thought as he reflected on the extent of the recent losses in their Lulu workforce. Inside one of the crystal domes, Ninmah's holographic image faded into view.

"Ninmah, it is now becoming *very* apparent that our Lulu workforce is encountering some drawbacks. Their life spans are coming to an end far earlier than anyone had anticipated, and many of them have expired as of late. Our gold yields are now beginning to suffer severely due to the fact that production has gone down dramatically!" Looking down at the floor, he mulled over their situation. "Replacement drones can in no way be reproduced fast enough, and a new campaign would be thoroughly implausible. Inevitably, this could be absolutely devastating to our operations."

He looked back up at her image with wide dilated eyes. "We must come up with an alternative solution...immediately!"

"I was concerned that this would one day become a issue, my lord," said Ninmah. "Subsequently, I have been doing some research into creating a more effective worker to do our mining. When our teams were excavating the pyramids on Mars, a number of objects were removed and archived into our libraries. Among the antiquities found, the teams discovered mummified bodies containing the DNA of beings that trace their origins back to the star system of Lira. After digging through our records, I did some tests on the catalogued artifacts and I believe that it is in this Lyrian DNA strand that the very answer we are looking for may lie."

Enki was intrigued. "Go on."

"We will be adding this highly developed Lyrian DNA to our already perfected Lulu design to clone a new being...a being that will be *thoroughly* capable of reproducing a workforce for us on its own." She paused as she looked over at Enki. "There *is* one small issue of concern though, my lord," she said.

Enki was quite intrigued with her plan for the new prototype, so if there *was* an obstacle, he would definitely want it addressed. He gave her a sideways glance. "So, what's the issue?"

"The creatures would be mammalian," she said, softly.

Enki frowned. "A mammal? Ninmah...I don't particularly care too much for the idea of our workforce being mammalian. No one would, really. You know quite well that they can be loud... smelly... and *very* unpredictable." He looked at her with narrowed eyes. "You are certain that this particular genetic combination would work?"

"I am very confident it *will* work," Ninmah told him.

He reached out and touched the large domed crystal with his sister's holographic image in it. "Enlil will not approve of this...so we won't tell him just yet. But I give you my complete authorization to proceed with the creating of this new mammalian workforce, dear sister. Come to the laboratories of the Abzu immediately so that we may proceed with this project unhindered and without scrutiny."

Ninmah bowed her head. "Your will be done, my lord. I will be aboard the next transport."

✦ ✦ ✦

Within the Ebineru genetic-science laboratory, trimmed in a black metallic substance, rows of tall, brightly lit, liquid-filled, cylindrical glass vats filled the room. The lab hummed with a dull throb as Enki and Ninmah studied their contents.

WOOOMM...WOOOMM...WOOOMM...

In various stages of development, cloned humanoid bodies floated in the large, clear vats, in a liquid solution of colloidal gold and highly oxygenated water. Recessed in the shadows, Ningishzida was busy monitoring them from one of the lab's many computer stations.

Before Ninmah and Enki, on oval lab tables, were two fully-developed male and female hominid beings set next to a series of crystalline computer monitors. The creatures had smooth, dark brown skin, with short, kinky black hair on their heads. Their bodies were sleek and muscular, elegant in their form and design.

Looking at their finished work, Ninmah told Enki, "I have decided to call these beings Human." She gestured toward the creatures.

"Their bodies are very resilient, having a highly adaptive metabolism, and they are capable of reproducing quite proficiently. These human beings will reproduce to create a most effective workforce for our mining operations in the Abzu within a very short period of time."

Enki looked the human creatures over thoroughly. "This is most pleasing news, sister."

She turned to Enki with a very serious look on her face. "The intellect of the human being is very strong though," she said, "and there is an element to this that has recently raised some *serious* concerns." She pointed at the nearby computer monitors, which displayed the holographic images of the human anatomy.

"The humans' brainwave patterns are at P.S.I. 1247 G9 MX-Alpha Gamma," she pointed out.

Squinting his eyes, Enki checked the readouts within the domed monitor, and he was absolutely shocked. "But Ninmah...how is this possible?"

"Well...the DNA from Lira is highly complex, and we have now combined it with our own highly complex DNA," she said as she looked over at the dormant humans behind them. "The result...is a being that is extremely complex and very highly developed. So highly developed that its higher brain functions enter the range of being potentially capable of not only shifting the vibrational form of matter but, according to these readings, if it so desired, it could very well possess the ability to influence the very fabric of time and space as well."

Enki was astounded. He had no idea this would be the result of their recent experiments. "Sister, this creature is much too powerful ... it must be destroyed!"

Ningishzida looked up from what he was monitoring and over at Ninmah as she bowed her head and was silent for a moment. "My lord, do not lose sight of our position. The success of our mission depends on these creatures," she said softly. "They have *all* the components we need to create our workforce." She looked at him and narrowed her eyes. "I believe the humans' bio-energy levels can be effectively dampened, therefore generating a much lower output. A series of blockages can be designed into the main central meridians channels of their energy fields. When we have these blockages in place, we will effectively be able to render the humans relatively harmless ... certainly docile enough to follow our orders."

Enki sighed. "Enlil will want this experiment terminated the moment he hears of it. We're dealing with a potentially very dangerous creature if it were ever to access its true nature."

"The three major gates that I will place along the creature's central energy channel will be virtually tamperproof and very effective. I will position the points here at the base of the neck, between the shoulder blades and here . . . at the base of the spine," she said, as she pointed at the hologram within the computer monitor.

The three of them continued studying the simulated images of human anatomy within the computer screens, as they conceived the designs for the placements of the fabricated energy blockages onto the human energy field.

Enki touched Ninmah on the arm. "You know that I have every confidence in you and your abilities in the arts of medical science, Ninmah. You will proceed with the application of the necessary dampening agents, and when the humans are ready, we will present our findings to the Great Council—together."

✦ ✦ ✦

The Anunaki laboratory was darkened except for the many small, dimly lit bay areas and the cylindrical glass vats with partial human bodies floating in them. The various stations were abuzz with activity, as gruesome stress tests were being performed on different parts of partial human anatomies.

In one of the bays, an open spinal cord was hooked up to many wires. Metal probes poked at various points along the spine's center. In another bay, a human liver floated in a glass vat that was hooked up to several jars by small, clear tubes; each of the jars containing a different brightly colored liquid.

In another one of the bays, the top half of a human head was hooked up from behind to a cluster of thin dark wires. On a small view screen positioned in front of it, there were rapidly flashing images of horrific things being projected continuously. From the corners of its lidless eyes, tears ran down the sides of the half face as it wept.

In the center of Enki's brightly lit laboratory, Ninmah stood on a small, black platform positioned above the two large, cylindrical glass tanks that contained the male and female humans. They floated submerged in a clear fluid, hooked up to a series of tubes and wires.

Ninmah was fully absorbed in the inspection of readouts within the computer monitors when Enki walked into the lab and came up the stairs next to the tank to join her on the platform. Without a word, she reached over and touched a small, blue crystal panel.

A mechanism within the tanks activated and the finished humans began to slowly rise from the large vats of hot water. As they rose from the tanks, gentle wisps of steam evaporated from their well-defined, dark, muscular bodies.

Enki looked over the finished humans closely. "I see that you have completed the final stages of blocking their central energies. Very good..." He looked at her. "Prepare them for transport imme-diately." He glanced over at the two humans. "I will inform the commanders of our coming and have them meet us in Eridu, where you and I will present our new workforce solution."

Ninmah acknowledged her brother's wishes and gently bowed her head respectfully.

Chapter Eleven

The large command center of Eridu was equipped with a full range of computer components that filled the room, as a variety of domed crystal monitors and many multi-colored crystal panels and buttons adorned the wealth of its many components. Lord Enlil was among the personnel of five commanders who were sitting at various stations throughout.

Marduk monitored transport activity as they all awaited the arrival of Enki and Ninmah, and when the shuttles were approaching within his monitors, he alerted the commanders.

"Sir, the transports are arriving from the Abzu," he announced.

"Very good," Enlil said. *I am quite eager to see these so called "humans" that Enki and Ninmah have created without sanction or any kind of actual approval,* he thought to himself.

Accompanied by two of his personal guards with Ninmah following closely behind, Enki and his entourage entered the large, domed Reception Hall within the great Water Palace of Eridu. A fine mist covered the dark marble floor of the large, plant-filled gallery as they escorted the two humans to the palaces' command center.

When they reached the control room, they stood before Enlil and the other assembled Anunaki commanders. "My lords," Enki said, as he gestured toward the couple. "These are the humans that I had informed you about, Adamu and Lilitu."

Enki stepped back to allow Enlil to come forward and inspect the creatures for himself, where he examined their physical make-up in great detail.

"Tell me something Brother... *why* would you add so much Rizqian and Lyrian DNA to your creation?" Enlil asked. He turned to Enki, and the look on his face was very serious. "I was *never* comfortable with the idea of playing God in the first place. You said this being already existed and that we would only need to put our mark upon it—They look nothing like us!"

Enlil began to raise his voice as he spoke to Enki. His tone was very angry. "You put the lives of all those Anunaki women in danger, including our sister and your own wife, Ninki! It was all to no avail; your handiwork was a failure." He looked over at creatures that they had created. "And now, you give *these* beings the ability to procreate by giving them our most complex genetic elements! Consider if they inherited our prolonged life cycles. This creature would easily overrun this planet in no time at all if it were allowed to!"

"Unfortunately, the Lulu in the Abzu have begun to expire long before we had anticipated." Enki explained calmly, "So, it was only out of sheer necessity that we have added this Lyrian DNA to our worker. In order to actually create a being capable of reproducing itself successfully, we have been *compelled* to create these mammalian hybrids," he explained, as he gestured toward the two humans. "You can be assured, we have taken extensive measures to dampen any access to much of the advanced components within their genetic makeup."

To give Enlil a better understanding of the project, Enki and Ninmah summoned Ningishzida from Ebineru to speak with him, so he could explain the human design further. He arrived at Eridu shortly thereafter and met with the Council of Commanders.

Ningishzida sat in the conference room with the commanders and explained more of the finer details of what they had created.

"Lord Enlil, the humans were given the power of procreation, but I assure you that they were *not* given the essence of prolonged life," he told him reassuringly, "We have taken care of that most effectively..."

"And really—what choice do we have?" Ninmah added. "End this mission in failure and leave all this Earth gold behind? Or to try and try again, to ultimately construct a worker being with the ability to reproduce itself?"

Angrily, Enlil gave in to the argument, "Fine!" he said, throwing his arms up. "Since they are obviously needed...you may use these beings in the Abzu as our workforce,"

Enki was relieved. "Very well then...we can begin their training by developing their basic service-related skills," he said. "They will be trained in the culinary arts of procuring and preparing food from our gardens so that they may tend to the dinner tables here in the Water Palace of Eridu." He watched Enlil's face for a reaction, but there was none.

Enlil continued to inspect the two beings and then turned to Ninmah. "What of the other potential threats these humans pose? Mammals can be known to be...unpredictable at times."

Enki answered for her, "Ninmah assures me that these creatures are under our complete control. Nevertheless...she and I plan to stay here in Eridu to monitor them while they adapt to their assigned duties and begin the reproduction of our new workforce."

Enlil turned to Enki and slowly stroked his chin whiskers as he nodded his head with a reluctant final approval.

Chapter Twelve

Within Edin's gardens, the Anunaki's knowledge of botanical sciences was extensive, and thoroughly astounding. With the combining of Siriun and Earth flora over the many years, a great range of bizarre and diverse plant life grew there, all preserved within its vast, enclosed estate. Against the backdrop of its lush green landscape, the garden was a colorful abundance of strange and unique vegetation and animal life that interacted with one another in a grand, harmonious perfection within the uniquely manicured rainforest jungle.

Many small rivers and streams wind throughout the lands, sharing their precious life force with plants and animals' alike, as an array of spectacular waterfalls and small pools complete the magnificent beauty of the garden paradise.

Life was pleasant and simple for the two new humans as they went about their assigned duties. There was always joy in their hearts, for they truly enjoyed what they did.

The human female Lilitu was eloquent in her mannerisms, as she gathered the exotic fruits and vegetables that grew naturally in the strange, lush botanical garden jungle. As she went about her duties, she was continuously in awe of the living beings of the forest. Almost all of the plant life, as well as most of the insects, birds and animals, had been brought to Edin from the Rizqian home world, their varieties and range of color being quite spectacular. Most of the flora and fauna were quite unique in their shape, size and function, as birds, animals, insects and plants all inter-acted in harmony with one another during their daily routines of dispersing different pollens and seeds throughout the lands, efficiently completing the intrinsic circuitry of the wondrous alien rainforest.

Lilitu put all the fruits and vegetables she gathered into a large woven basket she carried by a strap over her slim, dark brown shoulder. Sometimes when she walked past the strange plants, many of them would often respond to her presence and gently turn toward her, expressing a deliberate awareness and personality. She enjoyed their attention and would always make sure she was able to stop and say hello to them whenever she could.

In a nearby livestock pen, an exuberant Adamu fed cows, sheep, pigs, goats and a number of other strange looking domesticated animals from a small mobile food cart of straw and oats. The sun gleamed off the beads of sweat that covered his dark brown, muscular body, as he worked diligently at his duties. He enjoyed the animals very much and took very good care of them.

Often, while going about his different assigned chores and responsibilities within the gardens, he would smile a broad grin of wonder and excitement as he experienced new things.

Early one day while exploring the rainforest, he was able to witness firsthand the delicate circle of life that was constantly unfolding all around him within the Anunaki jungles of Edin's gardens. He found himself on one of the banks of the many rivers that wound through the estate and watched as small, colorful birds hunted flying insects from the safety of the many trees that hung over the water's edge. The birds would swoop down from trees and eat the bugs that flew near the water's surface.

Suddenly, a large, elongated fish with large teeth leapt out of the water and caught one of the colorful birds in its mouth for a meal of its own. Startled, Adamu was completely in awe of what he had witnessed.

Later, while hiding behind some bushes, he watched a cheetah as it coldly and methodically stalked and killed a gazelle-like creature. In silent admiration, he whispered, "Cheee...ta!" to himself as he pointed at the magnificent cat.

Enki had given Adamu the freedom to name anything he came across that he had not already been introduced to. He smiled—quite pleased with himself.

Later that evening, after all their duties had been attended to, Adamu and Lilitu went to their modest, cream-toned, domed stucco domicile. Inside, there was a small fireplace off to one side with a fire lit and a bed made of furs in the center of the room.

When they had settled in, Adamu begins to playfully chase Lilitu around the inside of their small home. Their playful game ultimately turns into a embrace that leads to a long, passionate kiss. The two young humans begin to explore each other's bodies with a sense of wonder and excitement that eventually turns into full-blown sexual abandon.

The couple seem to become one being, as they make love on the bed of furs long into the night. Hours later, after another explosive union, they lay in the furs holding each other closely. Breathing heavily, Lilitu, wide eyed and excited, stares up at the ceiling. Although their sex had been absolutely amazing, her mind was somewhere else.

"Adamu...I had the *most* wondrous day in the gardens today." She looked over at him with an excitement in her eyes that she couldn't contain. "The *plants*...they respond to my presence... they even *speak* to me!"

Adamu was perplexed. "How can a plant speak?" he said softly.

Lilitu recalled her experiences when she had been watering the Anunaki's sacred psychotropic plants of Sector R—of how she had walked among marijuana plants, opium poppies, and varieties of mushrooms, cocoa bushes and peyote button cacti. They all would gently turn toward her whenever she approached.

"It started out very subtle at first," she said. "The sacred plants of Sector R...the ones that Enki told us we were never to partake in. They beckoned me." She sat up and looked at him with wide eyes. "They whispered that they wished to share their sacred wisdom with me," she said, with a pleading tone in her voice. "I know it was wrong, but they bade I take them into me...I ate a mushroom." Adamu's eyes were wide as he lay there and looked at her, speechless. After a moment, she smiled softly as she looked back at him and continued. "The world around me seemed to change." Her eyes got wider and then narrowed as she explained what she had experienced, "Colors became more vivid and small sounds became clearer..."

In her mind, she remembered how the rainforest seemed to change into a pulsating living being and how it gently lit up with a soft glow that she and all the other living things around her seemed to be giving off. Lilitu sat looking up at the ceiling, unable to restrain her excitement as she recalled her psychedelic experience.

"I could sense and feel the energy of my entire body—and I saw how *everything* around me was alive, with consciousness and *intellect!*"

Adamu listened silently, in complete bewilderment.

"They showed me many secrets about myself...and the universe around us," she whispered. "They have awakened in me a *much* greater awareness!"

Adamu sat up, unhappy and confused. He looked at the floor. Lilitu watched him as he got up and stood next to the bed. He stared blankly at the wall, then looked over at her with a deep concern in his eyes.

"It is forbidden to partake in the Master's sacred plants. Lord Enki made this *very* clear to us!"

"But Adamu, my love," Lilitu pleaded. "These plants are special. They have shown me how to awaken my energies, to be like *Enki* and the other Elohim." She paused; a light sparkled in her eyes. "We *could* be like our creators...these sacred plants have shown me *how*."

Adamu was aghast and made a move to walk away from her, but Lilitu rushed from the bed to his side.

"Don't you see?" she asked. "I have somehow developed a unique relationship with these plants."

"This is madness...!" Adamu shouted. He gently pushed her away. "I tend to my duties, as well should you! I have no interest in establishing relationships with plants." He puffed out his chest and said proudly, "I seek only to observe the ways of the wild animals within the forest jungles, hone my skills in the hunt and to name all that is unnamed to us."

"Oh, Adamu," Lilitu said, "your day sounds so very exciting! I am interested in the ways of the wild as well." She grabbed him by the arm. "May I accompany you on your hunt? I promise I won't be a bother. It would be like I'm not even there!"

Adamu put his hand to his chin as he considered her request. *Perhaps that would take her mind off disobeying Enki's wishes,* he thought. "Well, I suppose you could join me. But silence and stillness are essential in the hunt...you must be sure not to spoil the trap," he said, sternly.

Lilitu was truly grateful and excited to be going with him. "Yes, Adamu, I promise." Looking at him with sultry eyes, she took him by the hand and led him back to bed to settle in for the rest of the night.

Resting with her head upon Adamu's chest as he fell fast asleep, she lay there wide-eyed and awake staring transfixed on the fire as it danced along the logs that were burning in the small fireplace. The firelight reflected in her large brown eyes, symbolized perfectly the fire of her newly awakened sense of ambition and inner desire for personal empowerment.

The next morning, Lilitu milled about the small domicile gathering the supplies that would be needed for the day's hunt. Adamu, still in bed, stretched as he opened his eyes. Lilitu looked over at him from beside the fireplace and smiled as she applied dark charcoal around her eyes.

"I am so thrilled that you are taking me on today's hunt," she said, as she prepared herself.

Adamu rubbed his eyes and got up. "Yes, well, let's eat and gather the extra supplies we'll need for the day. We must be on our way as *soon* as possible."

The two sit down at their eating table and have a small meal, then grab their supplies and head toward the door.

Throughout the course of their morning, Adamu teaches Lilitu how to hunt and she pays close attention to every detail. First, he teaches her how to fish and they experiment with putting worms on fishing hooks. He then shows her how to set small snares in the forest with chunks of raw meat, and at one point, they find themselves crouched silently in the bushes as he teaches her how to stalk prey. He finishes the mornings training by teaching her how to draw and fire a bow and arrow.

Lilitu mimics Adamu's stance perfectly as she stands next to him. Smiling, they aim their hunting bows at a small tree. In unison, they let their bowstrings loose. With a soft thud, their arrows hit the target with precision, Lilitu's arrow landing right next to Adamu's. She gives him a sly look and then laughs as they run over to retrieve them from their target. Lilitu had been enjoying the time she was spending with Adamu that morning quite a bit.

By midday, Adamu felt that he had taught Lilitu all he could and they agree to meet back up in a nearby clearing at the end of the day.

Heading off into the thick forest jungle, the two now go their separate ways, and when Lilitu finds that she is completely alone . . . she stops walking. Raising her arms and closing her eyes, she begins to establish a mental connection with the forest as she makes her intentions to harvest its bounty clear. After a few moments, three of the jungle's most proficient predators emerge from its shadows and come to her side to assist her—a large Dire wolf, a Mountain Lion and a Great Grey owl. She smiles softly to herself as she senses the power of their presence.

Lilitu opens her eyes slowly and continues smiling as she silently bonds with her new allies. She then takes her stance on the forest floor and places an arrow from her quiver in her bow as she looks into the jungle with narrowed eyes. Slowly... tree branches and vines of the thick jungle canopy begin to bend to the side and separate as the forest gently opens in on itself, exposing a number of different game animals as they graze peacefully.

She aims and fires. Her arrow makes a soft sound as it flies through the air and a dull thud as it hits a rabbit-like creature with an eloquent precision. She nods and smiles to herself with a great heartfelt satisfaction.

Lilitu quickly replaces the arrow in her bow as she starts to run through the forest. The tangle of vines and branches bend out of the way as she runs while firing her bow repeatedly... a quick and precise kill with each arrow released.

In the patchy shade of the forest, Adamu was consumed in the focus of the hunt as well. He spent his afternoon bow hunting, setting traps and placing fishing lines. At times, he would hide in the dense undergrowth, patiently and methodically stalking his game. When Adamu was on the move, he travelled gracefully through the forest, jumping and swinging from the many tangled vines and branches with a natural ease. Being a master of the bow, he made many kills when he used it.

As the sun began to cast its final rays, he was very proud of his day's catch, and he returned to the meeting spot they had designated in the small jungle clearing.

The light of the late afternoon sun lit up the leaves of the trees and grasses a bright vivid green and Lilitu was already there waiting for him at the clearing. She sat on the ground weaving a grass basket, looking rested and even a little bored. Proudly, Adamu stood before her and held up a reed rope that had a number of dead birds, small forest animals and fish hanging from it.

"Lilitu!" he said, with an unbridled excitement. "Behold… proud fruitful bounty of the forest!"

"Oh, Adamu," Lilitu said, "how wonderful. Observe *my* harvest of the forest's bounty!" She held up a similar rope of game in each of her hands and then gestured to some grass mats that she had woven, with eight additional ropes of game animals strung on them.

Adamu's jaw dropped. He was shocked and his face twisted with rage.

"Curse you, Woman!" he said, angrily. He pointed at her with narrowed eyes. "How *dare* you play this trick on me." His eyes widened. "You mock my prowess as a hunter!"

Lilitu looked bewildered. "But, Adamu, I—"

"Don't even speak to me! I will *not* deal with your strange behavior…and your strange ways!" He looked her up and down with narrowed eyes, and then got right up in her face.

"You mock me, and I will not have that!" He stepped back and with an arrogant look on his face, he said to her, "I leave you now, Woman, to reside among my brothers and sisters of the forest— the wolves." His eyes narrowed as he said under his breath, "For I find *their* loyalty to be…unquestionable!"

Lilitu was astounded as tears began to roll down her cheeks. She fell to her knees, crying softly over Adamu's distorted accusations and he walked off into the jungle without looking back.

Chapter Thirteen

L ater that week, back in the gardens, Lilitu was carrying her basket of gathered fruits and vegetables down a narrow path. Adamu carried a large bushel of wheat down the same path and was busy reminiscing of the time he had been spending with his new wolf family. He smiled to himself because they had recently accepted him as one of the pack. He was thinking back on the times that they had spent together, wrestling playfully, cleaning each other and taking care of each other's needs. As he passed Lilitu on the trail, he completely ignored her, almost bumping her off it as he passed her.

That evening, the two reported for their duties in the palace dining hall. On a long, sleek, white oval table, Lilitu had cut and arranged many different colorful fruits and vegetables into a variety of artistically expressive shapes and floral designs while Adamu artistically arranged cooked meats and vegetables on a large platter at the other end of the large table. Despite the pleasing arrangements, Lilitu looked sad and forlorn.

The two remained silent as they walked past each other and grabbed silver metal plates, bowls and goblets from a small cabinet built into the room's far wall and proceeded to set the long dinning room table.

Lilitu wondered if Adamu was still angry. She turned and got his attention, looking at him with inquisitive eyes. He quickly turned his head and put his nose in the air, and continued with his duties. Saddened, but more frustrated by his response, she looked down at the floor, but regained her composure and lifted her head as she tried not to let it affect her.

After they had finished their tasks, the two walked to separate ends of the room and stood at attention with their backs to the walls, eyes forward, hands clasped in front.

The main doors swung open abruptly and a group of reptilians entered the hall. They spoke among themselves as they settled into the chairs around the large table and proceeded to dig into the sumptuous feast that had been prepared for them.

When the meal was over, the two humans cleaned up the mess in silence as Adamu ignored Lilitu. After they had finished, he went off on his own. Lilitu glared at him as he left. She felt that it was odd that he would rather spend his time with the beasts of the forest than with her.

Adamu spent that evening on a high bluff, watching the sunset with one of the female wolves of the pack that he had bonded with, outside of a den that they shared. When the sun had completely dipped behind the horizon, the two retired to their secluded sleeping quarters for the rest of the evening.

✦ ✦ ✦

The next morning, in the science labs of Eridu, two of the Anunaki scientists were discussing the humans as they observed their actvities within their domed, crystalline view monitors. One of them reached over and pressed an orange crystal panel on the computer console to hail Lord Enki. Within moments, his image appeared inside one of the monitors.

"My lord," the lab assistant said, as he lowered his gaze and tipped his head, "There appears to be a development with the male human. It seems that he does not want to mate with his female counterpart and is currently living with a pack of wolves in the Forest Sector 93B19."

"This *is* most peculiar," Enki said. "Acknowledged. Take no action...I will see to this issue personally."

By midday, Enki was walking down the lush, well-manicured, jungle trail that brought him to a clearing with a small structure within it. Set off to the edge of the small field, he approached the modest, thatched roof, food-and-refreshment kiosk. It's rough, high-pitched grass roof concealed small countertops, cupboards and seating modules. When he reached it, he touched a small panel that activated a hidden loudspeaker.

TOOKI—TOOKI—TOOKI!

Enki walked over to a small refrigerator and pulled out some fruit. In a small blender, he mixed them into a liquid beverage and then sat down to enjoy his drink as he waited for Adamu to arrive.

"Hello, my lord. It's so nice to see you today!" a voice said from behind him. Enki turned around to see the male human approaching from the other side of the small clearing.

When he got there, Adamu sat down on the stool next to the large reptilian commander, and looked up at him with a furrowed brow.

"I'm glad you're here father. I have been wanting to speak with you about the possibility of finding me a new mate," he began.

Enki was rather surprised by the request. He turned to him and asked, "Adamu, my son. . . why would you want a new mate?"

"This one," Adamu said with venom in his voice, "mocks my prowess as a hunter and provider!"

"Now just a moment Child," Enki was very stern in his conviction. "The female human was made for you to mate with. You will mate with her—no exceptions!"

Knowing better than to question Enki's command, Adamu was sullen as he looked at the ground. "Yes, Lord Enki, my father . . . my creator. I shall do as you wish."

Shortly after their meeting, Adamu returned to his modest garden domicile and went inside, where he was greeted by a quite visibly repulsed Lilitu.

"What do *you* want?" she said with disdain.

Adamu slowly and silently approached Lilitu. He paused to pull off the leather loincloth he was wearing and then continued his advances, his naked muscular brown body coming toward her slowly with no sign of relent.

"Get away from me!" Lilitu hissed, pushing him back.

Adamu grabbed Lilitu around the waist and pulled her close. She struggled to get away.

"No...! I will not share my body with you!" she shouted. "You share your body with the beasts of the forest. We are *not* like them, or of them. You disgust me!"

Adamu released her. He then pointed to the bed with a stern look on his face.

"You *will* mate with me," he growled.

Lilitu crossed her arms and turned her head. "Humph!"

Adamu grabbed Lilitu by the arm and forced her down onto the bed of fur and pillows. He grabbed her by the hands and pushed her into the bedding, and then proceeded to forcefully penetrate her from behind. She could not move and tears rolled down her face as she cried. Adamu held Lilitu down as he continued to rape her for what seemed like forever. After much relentless abuse, he finally released his seed in an intense climax and passed out on top of her immediately afterward.

Lilitu looked around desperately as she struggled to remove herself from under her incoherent assailant without awakening him. In time, she was able to wriggle out from underneath him, and she ran for the door.

Fleeing their small residence in the dim light of the waning moon, Lilitu ran toward the distant palace of Eridu, sobbing as tears rolled down her face. She got to the palace and ran down the long entry corridor, high above the wide waterway that surrounded it. A large, light green-skinned palace guard stood at its massive round entrance and by the time she had reached him, she was hysterical.

"Where is Enki?" she screamed. "I must speak to him at once! Where is he...!?"

The guard just looked at her. He walked over to a nearby command console imbedded in the wall and touched a purple crystal panel.

"My lord, the human female is here, and there seems to be some sort of situation." He looked over at Lilitu. "It appears to be very upset and is requesting your immediate presence. Are you available sir?"

"Yes..." Enki's voice could be heard over the speaker. "I'll be right there." The speaker went silent and the guard returned to where Lilitu was waiting.

"Lord Enki has heard your request," the guard said coldly. "Wait here and he will be with us shortly."

The massive round palace entranceway soon opened from its center and there, wearing a dark green hooded cloak, stood Enki.

As soon as she saw the Anunaki commander, Lilitu ran over to him. Sobbing, she clung tightly to his side.

Enki looked down at the young human female and pushed her back gently. He suggested that they sit down, as he motioned toward a small metallic bench in a recessed corner of a nearby courtyard area filled with swampy mist and surrounded by many varieties of lush alien plant life.

"Now...what seems to be troubling you, my child?" he asked calmly.

Lilitu's eyes welled up with tears as she looked up at Enki and sobbed, "It's your Adamu creature...It—it has been sharing its body with the beasts of the forest, but we are not like them!" She softly cried as she turned away from him shamefully. "I find it to be absolutely disgusting that he wanted to mate with me, and I refused him because of it...then, he *attacked* me. He physically forced himself upon me and raped me, my lord!" She looked into Enki's eyes, pleading. "Please Master, take me from his reach."

Lilitu reached out and gently touched the large lizard man on his scaled cheek as she looked at him with a gentle admiration. "The

beast Adamu is nothing like *you* my lord, so noble, so wise, so...
handsome."

Enki was quite surprised by Lilitu's directness. He glanced at her
with narrowed eyes as he stroked his chin whiskers contemplatively, for he found himself experiencing a strong sense of arousal
being brought on by her subtle seduction. Finally, he spoke.

"I have decided...to remove you from the gardens and your
duties there," he said to her in an authoritative tone. He reached
out and grabbed Lilitu gently by the shoulders as he looked deep
into her eyes. "You will now be known as *Lilith*, and you will
accompany me. You will come live aboard my orbiting space
station, as my personal consort."

Lilith's eyes lit up at the suggestion and she smiled. "My lord...
that sounds wonderful!"

✦ ✦ ✦

High above the Earth, onboard the now shut down Anunaki
space station; Enki and Lilith sit together looking out over the
planet. The modular seating area that they lounge in is recessed
into the floor and accommodates soft, dark brown leather couches
that face large bay windows. Dressed in sleek and sexy Anunaki
consort attire, Lilith wears a scant black outfit and a headdress
made of the black horns of a gazelle, her dark brown arms and
thighs adorning black horned bands that compliment spiked
shoulder pads and a small tapered bikini top.

As they relax, casually taking in the spectacular view above
planet Earth, Enki slowly repositions himself behind Lilith and
begins to caress her delicate, dark brown face with his scaly, clawed
finger. With a heightened sense of passion and arousal, he takes
her and mounts her forcefully. She welcomes it, lifting her leg and
turning her body so that they can face each other. She touches him
and smiles with wide eyes as he enters her. Lying back, she closes
her eyes and moans softly.

Lilith was now where she felt she truly belonged...finally.

Back in Edin, when Adamu had finished his day's work, to his dismay, he came home to an empty house. Lilitu was gone when he woke up that morning and he had assumed she had left early to go to work. But he hadn't seen her all day...and considering she wasn't home by now, Adamu felt his heart sink into his stomach. He knew now that she was really gone, and he was furious.

Adamu stormed out of the small domicile and headed toward the grandiose silver palace of Eridu to tell Enki. Upset and confused, he ran up the Water Palace's long entry corridor and angrily addressed the guard who was standing watch.

"Where is Lord Enki?" he bellowed as he tried to catch his breath. "I must speak with him at once!"

The guard just looked down at him, "And what exactly is so important that you request I disturb my lord?" the guard asked.

"It is my female...Lilitu. She is missing!"

"As you wish," the guard said unsympathetically. "I will inform Lord Enki, and *you* will wait for his response in this courtyard." He motioned toward the side area and Adamu grudgingly walked over and sat down on the metal bench.

After waiting a very long time, Enki finally appeared at the palace entranceway. Anxiously, Adamu jumped to his feet and ran over to him.

"My lord...! The female Lilitu. She's gone!"

Enki looked at him blankly. "Yes, my child, I know...I have removed her from the gardens. She now resides aboard my space station—as my personal consort."

Adamu's eyes widened upon hearing the shocking news. His jaw clenched up and his nostrils flared, as tears welled up in his eyes.

"But why, Father? Why have you done this...? Didn't you tell me that Lilitu was *my* mate, created specifically for me?" He was angry and grew defiant as he said under his breath, "I curse you for coveting my mate—Lord Enki, son of Anu!" He teared up again. "How could you do this?" he sobbed.

Enki closed his eyes and shook his head. "Curse not foolishly...
and be calm, my child," he said softly. "The female Lilitu was
dangerous." He put his hand on Adamu's shoulder. "She would
have hurt you, Adamu. I have removed her from the gardens to
protect you."

Adamu shrugged off Enki's hand. "Lord Enki," he said. "Return
my mate at once!"

Enki continued to be patient with him. "Adamu, my son...I am
providing you with a *new* mate."

Adamu's right eyebrow rose, as if he didn't quite believe what he
had just heard.

"Yes, my child...a new mate." He extended his hand and gestured down a nearby corridor. "If you wish, you may accompany
me to witness the creation of this new mate."

Adamu looked down the long silver corridor, then back at Enki
and nodded approvingly as he regained his composure and wiped
away his tears.

Chapter Fourteen

As Adamu entered the genetics laboratory of Eridu with Enki, he was amazed. The soft drone of machines filled the large room.

WOOOMM…WOOOMM…WOOOMM…

There were human body parts connected to wires floating in clear fluid inside of large clear vats. Some of the body parts seemed to move and twitch on their own, and this made him more than a little uneasy.

Enki brought Adamu over to a large open tank filled with a dark brown liquid. He reached down and touched a small panel under a monitor attached to the edge of the tank and silently, an incomplete human body slowly rose up from the dark liquid. It was apparent that the skin and many of the muscles on the body had not developed all the way yet.

Adamu was absolutely disgusted at what he was being shown. He looked at Enki with wide eyes and asked him, "Lord Enki, you expect me to *mate* with this horrific creature?"

Enki said nothing at first as he calmly studied the tank's data printouts. He finally responded, "I assure you my son…she will look much different when she is done."

Adamu shook his head, not believing what he was looking at. He looked around the room, "I wish to leave this place at once… I want nothing to do with this madness!"

Enki calmly bowed his head as he gestured toward the door and they departed the strange alien laboratory. Adamu was glad for it. The experience had made him uncomfortable and left him feeling more horrified and confused than enlightened.

✦ ✦ ✦

Onboard the orbiting space station, in the captain's quarters, Enki sat in the command chair with Lilith by his side. He was working in front of a crystalline view monitor at a computer console and she was relaxing, submerged in a hot tub made from the pearlescent shell of a large sea creature embedded into the ship's floor. Wearing nothing but a black horned headdress and horned armbands, Lilith was also engrossed as she worked on a small computer monitor of her own.

A look of frustration suddenly came across her face and she looked over at Enki. Rising from the steamy waters slowly, Lilith stepped out of the hot tub as a fine mist evaporated from the skin of her elegant, dark brown body. Sauntering seductively over to Enki, she gently climbed up on him and settled herself onto his lap. She smiled softly as she reached out and gently stroked his smooth, scaled face and chin whiskers, slowly looking up at him with a soft allure.

"My lord... my life here with you pleases me greatly, and your sciences are *so* powerful." He turned from what he was doing and gave her his attention. "We, are now as we *should* be... equal above all others," she said, stroking his arm. "Show me, my lord; show me the deeper secrets of your sciences. My access to files I have been studying recently concerning molecular gravity, pyrokinetics and many of the other secrets of your higher sciences, have been blocked."

Enki looked at her and said nothing. He had blocked the files and was beginning to get irritated with her constant questions. Lately, she had even been hinting at holding a significant position in their Earth operations... and that was simply not going to happen.

Lilith grew agitated.

"I *long* to know their secrets," she said, persistently. "Are they not my birthright?" Her tone turned accusatory as she looked him square in the face. "I am...just like you!" she said, as she slowly began to fully realize the underlying truth of the matter.

Caught off guard by the audacity of Lilith's bold accusations, in his mind's eye he could feel his sister's thoughts, whispering in his ear... *she knows!*

He abruptly shoved Lilith off his lap and onto the floor. Curling his lip and narrowing his eyes, he looked down at her with disdain.

"You are *not* my equal... you are not like me," he uttered. "I am your creator—your God—!" He gave her a hard look. "You will leave this place now. I banish you from my sight and from *all* of my technologies!" He reached over to a command console and pushed a small panel. "Guard!"

A large reptilian guard responded immediately to the call, and stood inside the room's doorway. "My lord?"

"Transport the human female to the Earth's surface... and leave her in the middle of the desert," Enki said. "She will no longer be welcome in Edin." He glared at Lilith. "Remove her from my sight!"

The Siriun guard walked over to Lilith where she sat on the floor completely stunned by Enki's response. He reached down and picked her up by the arm to take her off the ship. Saddened and confused, with tears in her eyes, she looked back at Enki, astounded as the guard abruptly escorted her through the dark, metal doorway.

Chapter Fifteen

Enki stood in the jungle clearing at the small refreshment kiosk, accompanied by a fully developed human female who was an exact replica of Lilitu. She stood next to Enki, doe-eyed and naked as he reached over and pressed a panel in the kiosk to activate the loudspeaker that would call Adamu.

TOOKIE—TOOKIE—TOOKIE!

Adamu soon emerged from the jungle and perched himself in a nearby tree. Arrogantly, he stood there on the branch and looked down on them.

"Lord Enki...so *this* is the creation who is to be my new bride? She appears to be no different than the old one."

Adamu jumped down from the tree branch, circled and sniffed the myterious new female, then lifted his head up to look at Enki. Suddenly, he leapt away and climbed back up into the trees again.

"No disrespect my lord, but this woman reeks of the madness of your sciences," he shouted down to them. "I will not name her... I will not mate with her...I will have nothing to do with her."

Adamu then jumped from the tree branch above them and quickly disappeared back into the thick interior of the rain forest jungle.

Enki, extremely displeased with his response, reached down and picked up the human female. Draping her over his shoulder like a rag doll, he turned and headed back toward the palace of Eridu.

When Enki returned to the genetics laboratory, he set the complacent human female down on one of the exam tables. With an aggravated exhale, he looked up and balled his fist.

"Uhhhaaaaaaahh!"

From out of a darkened area of the lab, Ninmah spoke, startling him. "Problems with the new female, my brother?" she asked cryptically, as she slowly emerged from the shadows.

"The human females are very complex creatures!" he snapped. "And...the male human has now *rejected* his new mate!"

Ninmah came closer. "I suppose you would know of the complexity of the human female, my lord, having recently taken the creature as your personal consort and then ultimately rejecting her as well," she said slyly. Looking at her, he did not respond.

Ninmah quickly disregarded the question and returned to the topic at hand. "So, tell me...why has the male rejected his new female?"

Taking a deep breath, he exhaled dramatically, "I don't know... I can only assume that the series of recent events have left him somewhat...scarred." He looked at Ninmah blankly. "He tells me that this new female reeks of our sciences, and that he will have nothing to do with her."

"My lord, the mammalian mind is *governed* by emotion, as you well know. It must have been very unsettling for this creature to see his new bride in her unfinished state." She went to the command console, grabbed a blue Mae Stone from a number of crystals that were set into a small tray and placed it into the central panel. Turning to one of the large monitors, she examined the readouts. "The male has also been threatened by its first mate's excessive ambitions and personal prowess." She looked back over her shoulder at Enki. "The replacement female must have been seen as a similar threat."

She motioned toward the viewing dome. Inside the crystalline monitor, a transparent hologram of the female brain appeared with a thermal image of the areas where enhanced brain activity was taking place.

"Notice the enhanced synaptic firing in the cerebral cortex of the female brain." The frontal lobe of the brain within the monitor was completely lit up in a reddish glow.

"This enhanced brain activity is what is creating the higher sense of ambition in our human female. It seems the female brain functions with a complexity that is not found in the male brain."

Enki thought about it for a moment and then turned to his sister. "Ninmah...it is apparent that we need to make the female human more like the male. *It* seems to be thoroughly capable of following orders and tending to its assigned duties."

"I agree, and...I have come up with a solution," Ninmah said. Inside the monitor, a transparent hologram of the male human's anatomy spun slowly next to the female brain as a series of chemical strands unraveled from the image of the female brain.

"We can effectively dilute this original human female design by creating a female clone from the stem cells of its male counterpart." The monitor showed Adamu's lower rib coming away from his body as the stem cells contained within it became magnified.

"The creature's rib bone can be easily removed without causing any kind of significant damage to its physiology. We can then synthesize stem cells gathered from the bones marrow." She turned to face Enki. "This new human female should ultimately prove to be a *much* easier being to control."

Enki stroked his chin whiskers as his eyes narrowed. "This is a most satisfactory solution...you have done well Ninmah," he said. "I give you my consent to proceed with the creation of this new, redesigned human female."

Enki walked over to the young woman whom Adamu had just rejected. He looked at her as he cradled her head in his large reptilian hand, gently touching her smooth, delicate brown face.

"Just look at her, Sister. Potentially so powerful...yet they're so..."

Suddenly he snapped the girl's neck with a precise twist. She went limp and fell to the table, dead. He looked up at his sister.

"Delicate," he said, coldly.

"Yes," Ninmah said, "this original human female design is very driven to awaken what we have worked so hard to dampen and dismantle. And yet...they are extremely delicate." She paused to look at Enki and cocked her head slightly, narrowing her eyes.

"So tell me, my lord," she continued, "how *did* you dispose of your...recent consort?"

Enki continued to stare at the lifeless female corpse a moment before he responded. "For some reason"—he turned to Ninmah—"I could not find it in myself to destroy her, so I have decided to let the Earth consume her. I have sent her to the middle of the desert...to perish."

Chapter Sixteen

The small shuttlecraft lands in the desert amidst a cloud of dust. As it settles, the craft's bay door opens and a small metallic ramp extends down to the ground. Wearing a black horned headdress, arm and leg bands, and a scant, sexy, shimmery aqua blue consort outfit, Lilith is accompanied by a large, tan reptilian guard who escorts her down the ramp by the arm. At the end of the ramp, he coldly pushes her off it into the sand. The guard then turns, and goes back up the ramp and back into the ship. The door closes behind him and the craft lifts off in another large cloud of dust, leaving Lilith alone in the middle of a vast, barren desert.

As Lilith stands up, she covers her face with her arm as a shield, her eyes squinting from the intense light of the midday sun. She looks around at the barren desert for a moment, then up at the blazing sun. In despair, Lilith falls to her knees and holds her head in her hands as she softly weeps.

When she had fully exhausted her tears, Lilith composes herself as she removes her horned headdress and wipes the tears away. Taking in her surroundings with a more level head, she was now able to focus on the full ramifications of her dire situation.

She ultimately comes to the conclusion that she would need to immediately protect herself from the searing rays of the sun first and foremost, so she begins to dig a trench. When she has finished digging, she breaks off one of the large horns from her headdress to use as a breathing tube and then begins to bury herself in the cool desert sand.

Lilith finds her forced stillness to be very confining but quite necessary, as not to be crushed by the desert sand that surrounds her. In time, she eventually gives in to her feelings of claustrophobia and falls into a deep, meditative slumber.

The night desert is lit by the light of a half moon, as Lilith slowly rises from the desert floor. The fine graduals of sand gently fall from her body as she stands up and looks to the heavens. She studies the stars of the night sky to get an idea of where north is located, in order to figure out which direction she should start traveling. When she is convinced of the desert's orientation, she closes her eyes and mentally envisions the ocean waters that lay far to the west of her. Her mental image begins to travel over the vast desert sands until it ultimately reaches the ocean's sparkling waters. Under the light of a full moon, the vision begins to travel rapidly over the ocean's shimmering green surface and then suddenly, it plunges down into the dark watery depths. Lilith is completely in awe as she witnesses the vast abundance of sea life that swims all around her.

The ocean is now to be her destination. Ripping a piece of cloth from her outfit, she lashes the black horn over her shoulder and begins her long trek toward the distant horizons lying to the west.

As Lilith walks into the night, eventually, the rays of the morning sun slowly begin to touch her face. She stops walking and gets down on her knees and she begins to dig herself another trench.

While buried and lying perfectly still, in Lilith's mind, every thing slowly fades to nothing. From within the dark recesses of her mind, a point of light slowly begins to expand. As the light expands, it turns into a vision of herself—surrounded by a bright, blue aura, and she finds herself floating in a vast field of stars.

Lilith listens closely as the sound of her heart rate begins to slow down.

THUMP, THUMP. . . THUMP. . . . . . THUMP. . . . .
THUMP. . . . . THUMP

The sun's final rays fade from the desert floor and Lilith rises from the earth, her dark skin and lips have now begun to dry and crack. She begins her journey west, but stops for a moment. With her fingernail, she digs into a fleshy part of her hand and sucks on the blood that comes from the small wound that she has created, and she feels a little better.

Feeling her spirit strengthen somewhat, she continues to walk across the darkened desert floor toward her destination, driven by what she knows lay past the distant horizon. She walks all night and when the rays of the rising sun begin to touch the desert floor, she lies down and buries her body in the sand once again.

In the long shadows of the setting sun, Lilith rises from the sand of desert floor, her skin now terribly dry and cracked. . . the lack of food and water having absolutely ravaged her.

As she slowly stands up, she reflects on how vivid her visions had been becoming. It was almost as if she had been in a waking dream, her mind now having gained the ability to rise up out of her body and move about in her immediate surrounding environment.

Not long after she had begun her long walk into the night, she stops suddenly. Closing her eyes, she clutches her stomach in pain as she falls to her knees and her body miscarries a small fetus onto the sand. Bewildered, Lilith looks at the bloody mass in the light of the moon, not sure exactly what to make of it.

Although she is half delirious, her face lights up and she slowly begins to smile. Picking up the fetus . . . Lilith quickly puts it to her lips and consumes it with a savage hunger.

After she had finished the small blessing of sustenance, she gets up and continues her walk into the cool desert night under the light of the new moon. Tonight she would have a slightly renewed sense of strength and stamina as she trudges west, across the darkened desert floor.

Finding herself buried in the sand of the desert floor once again, Lilith's visions have become very strong and are as vivid as a waking dream. She leaves her body and sees herself floating in the sand of the desert floor. Her thoughts begin to focus on the center of her forehead and then travel inside of her head, into her mind's eye. There, in a kind of polarized, negative imagery that gives off a soft glow, Lilith sees imagery of the area of the desert she is in and the surrounding land masses for miles around. The landscape below her begins to accelerate faster as she began to travel over it rapidly in her mind's eye. When she reaches the ocean's coastline, her vision flies low and fast over the dark, moonlit waters.

Lilith was now beginning to fully master her natural ability of— Far Sight.

After another long night of walking, Lilith buries herself in the sand once again, except this time she is able to simply lie down on the ground and softly wriggle her body down into it. Lilith shimmies her entire body into the desert floor and then falls into a deep slumber.

Just as the night before, she sees herself floating in a sea of sand. Her mental vision slowly travels into her own ear and she can see the molecules within her eardrum as they vibrated.

TZINGGGGG... WA AH AH AHHHHH...

Her vision then slowly pulls out of her ear canal and into the surrounding sand particles. The vibration of the sand makes a distinct sound.

NNANGHHHHHH... NNANGHHHHHH...

The vision that Lilith sees of her own body now begins to fuzz. When it refocuses, she sees that her body has become made entirely of desert sand. She successfully has altered her bodies vibration—

and physically changed it to that of the desert sand she is immersed in.

Lilith had *now* begun to master her intrinsically unique ability of—Earth Melding, truly becoming one with the mighty desert that would have otherwise consumed her. She meditated quite peacefully that day.

When Lilith rose from the desert's floor that evening, she felt somewhat recharged, but ravaged nonetheless. Walking into the darkened desert, she heads toward its familiar western horizon. Lilith had only traveled for a short while when she begins to hear a faint sound in the distance. Lifting her head, she listens closer. It is the ocean. As she walks farther, the sound becomes louder.

WOOOOSH......WOOOOSH......WOOOOSH......
WOOOOSH......

She smiles softly to herself, as she begins a struggled run for the ocean waters off in the darkened distance. Finally, she comes to the edge of a bluff and makes a struggled climb down to its moonlit coastal shoreline. There, she stops and breathes in the fresh, salty ocean air deeply.

Needing fresh water to drink immediately, she closes her eyes to meditate on what she should do. In her mind, she envisions the landscape of the local area in the light of negative imagery where all shadows give off a soft glow. She sees the shoreline she is on, alongside the dunes and cliffs of the ocean's coastline. In her vision, she sees a freshwater spring running down a nearby cliff wall.

Opening her eyes abruptly, she turned and quickly headed in the direction of the sacred waters.

Lilith soon reached the small spring and she fell to her knees. With a desperate sense of relief and renewal, she cupped some of the water trickling from the cliff wall in her hands and drank long and deep of its life giving essence. When she finally had her fill of the precious fluid, she laid back onto the sand and quickly fell into a deep slumber.

Chapter Seventeen

When Lilith awakens, the rays of the morning sun almost blind her, as the ocean waves pound loud and powerful against the coastal shoreline. Squinting, she covers her eyes with her arm and tries to look around. As she stands up and shades her eyes with her hand, she looks out over the vast ocean waters. With her hand clutching her stomach, hunger is now her only immediate concern. Narrowing her eyes, she thinks to herself about the great bounty that swims hidden, just below the water's surface.

Turning from the sea, Lilith climbs to the top of the rocky, coastal cliff line. With no hesitation of any kind, she faces the ocean and begins a full force run toward the cliff's edge. Reaching the precipice, she jumps from the high cliff and does a graceful swan dive into the brightly gleaming ocean waters.

The moment her body hits the water, she feels the sensation of dissipating into an egg-flower like mass. As it slowly fades, she begins to feel like she is back in her body once again. Floating gently below the water's surface...Lilith now breathes in with newly formed gills. Looking at her hands and feet, she discovers that she has morphed webbing as well. With narrow-eyed scrutiny, she slowly looks around with a predatorial reserve, and in an instant, she turns and swims swiftly down into the depths of the dark blue ocean waters as she initiates her hunt, killing and eating fish and other sea life with a fierce voracity.

With the ocean waters teaming with life, Lilith is quite proficient as she attacks her prey with a cunning precision and accuracy...the hunt going on long into the morning hours; kill after kill, after kill.

Once satiated, Lilith is finally able to relax peacefully in her new underwater environment. The sensation being much like floating in space, she feels her mind awaken to its magical potential. She experiences the sensation of her body morphing once again into a creature of the sea that was no longer smooth, having horns and spikes along her body, much like that of a Lionfish.

As she takes a moment to relax, she looks around in her strange, new underwater environment casually, and reflects upon all she has achieved. Smiling softly to herself, she begins to laugh at the fact she has remained undaunted, in spite of the many obstacles she has overcome.

Slowly, a wealth of sea life begins to gather all around her. There are creatures of many varieties and spectacular colors. The blue green waters are now filled with the blues and yellows of tropical fish and the oranges and reds of eels and jellyfish. It doesn't take her long to notice that the sea life all around her seemed to swim and move in accordance with her thoughts and body movements.

The phenomena starts out slowly at first...then begins to spread to all the creatures gathered around her. In time, a grand perform-ance of fish ensues. Creatures, such as shark, rainbow fish, eel, dolphin, jellyfish, tuna, and sardine—they all swam intertwined, with a unique and unnatural precision, creating many different amazing and colorful, geometric patterns.

New life burst forth, as baby sea creatures are born from many of the beings, all in an orchestrated procession. The crab and shrimp dance around her on the ocean floor in intricate patterns that compliment the colorful display that unfolds above them with brilliant splendor. Smiling softly to herself, Lilith sits there for hours gently waving her arms as she conducts the life orchestra that swims all around her in a magnificent expression of unique and unnatural precision.

Throughout the days during her life within the oceanic world, Lilith spent much of her time exploring her new, underwater kingdom. At times, her body would chameleon and change, taking on the physical characteristics of her environment to camouflage and blend in with its aesthetic. In this state, she was able to learn much about the creatures of the sea and of their life below the water's surface.

One day, within the depths of the dim green waters, Lilith lounged peacefully on the sandy ocean floor accompanied by six large sea eels that she had befriended as companions. As she lay among them in a meditative state, with an absence of any thoughts in particular, she stared at the water's surface, far in the distance. As she stared blankly into the dark green void of her underwater world, an ominous image began to take shape. The shadow image above her slowly began to resemble that of Lord Enki, with vividly accurate detail. She thought about Enki and his people and she realized that the creatures she had been spending her time with, as intelligent as they were, were as children compared to the intellect of her creators, the Anunaki. Lilith longed for the company of beings of higher intellect and quickly became bored with her newfound kingdom.

In her mind, a vision flashes of the mainland from out at sea. A negative image of the coastline appeared in her head and the vision begins to travel quickly over the ocean waters. Off in the distance, a sleekly spired Anunaki castle sat nestled into the rocky cliff line. The image begins to fill her mind as the vision travels closer and closer to the gothic palace. After a moment, Lilith cleared her head. She knew now what she needed to do.

With sadness, Lilith says goodbye to the creatures she had become so close to and then swims off toward the distant coastal shorelines.

The golden rays of the low, setting sun cast an illuminated glow behind Lilith's pale brown body as she slowly rises from the ocean waters. Wearing a scant bikini-style outfit, her headdress and shoulder guards are made of seaweed and the spiny, horned shells of sea creatures, eloquently stylizing the spines and horns of the beings that she perpetually wished to emulate, her horned creators—the Anunaki.

Rising from the ocean waters, she walked slowly toward the sandy beach, her gills and webbing melting away from her body as she returned to the land above the world she knew within the sea.

By the time Lilith reached the shoreline, all she could think about was meeting the relatives of Enki whom she had only heard about in stories. They were a part of the Anunaki elite who had recently come to the newly developed world of Earth for more leisure oriented reasons than the groups before them who, through necessity, had been focusing purely on the attainment of gold for the healing of their home world.

Climbing to the top of the bluff, she turned toward the ocean and took a deep breath as she appreciated the brilliancy of the final rays of a day's sunset once again. Lilith was enchanted by the magnificence of its beauty as the sunset lit up the sky with rich hues of orange, soft purple and pink. When the sun had gone, she turned away from the horizon and focused on the task of reaching her Anunaki hosts. Looking around, she picked up a large branch to use as her walking staff and she adorned it with a few random shells, bird skulls and feathers. With a rekindled spirit and a bold sense of adventure, Lilith turned toward her destination and headed off along the path on her journey to find Enki's brethren.

After a short while, travel along the narrow cliff's darkening pathway became awkward and even dangerous, so Lilith found a nice spot in a small, recessed grassy area, where she lay down and quickly fell asleep for the rest of the night.

Lilith awoke early the next morning with the rising sun. It was grey, cloudy and lightly raining along the coastal shoreline. The moisture felt good on her skin as she got up and stretched out before she began the day's journey.

During her travels along the dirt path among the rocky crags, she found herself wanting to practice her magic, but being on land was a very different sensation than that of the weightless under-water world she had become accustomed to. Her mind felt heavy and distracted by the physical world around her, and her magic was not as powerful now. She would need to concentrate on the simpler aspects of her art, like her psychokinetic abilities.

When it was time to rest, Lilith sat down along the trail and began to focus her mind on stimulating the molecules within a small tree that had fallen near the path. After a moment, a wisp of smoke began to rise from the log and she successfully managed to ignite a small fire. Pleased with her results, she warmed herself by the heat of its flame. When she felt rested, she got up and con-tinued on her way along the narrow path.

It was late afternoon and Lilith had been walking most of the day along the rocky cliff line. The sun hung low in a cloudy sky as she travelled along its windy bluff. The path she had been follow-ing now began to narrow abruptly and then, from around a corner, a massive stone palace loomed omniously before her. The logo of Lord Astarte's house adorned the large arched stone entranceway of the immense Rizqian castle as it sat nestled among the rocky cliff line.

A huge, round, dark metallic doorway dominated the castle's entranceway as large quartz crystal formations grew from the rocks at each of its sides. The symbol above the door was a grey steel triangle with blunted tips, its inner pattern being drawn toward the center from its consecutive edges, forming the inner image of a reticulated iris.

As Lilith approached the palace entranceway, she stopped and looked up at the crest hanging above the great doorway. This was the ocean castle estate of Lord Astarte, one of the Anunaki Elite and cousin of Lord Enki. She raised her cupped hands to her mouth and called out.

"Lord Astarte! It is I... Lilith! Creation of Lord Enki," she announced proudly.

"I have been wandering these lands for many days!" She paused for a moment, then looked back up and announced, "I seek refuge ...and the company of beings of intellect." She raised her arms and shouted, "Will you have me?"

A hologram appeared inside one of the large, natural quartz crystals next to the doorway. It was Lord Astarte. She recognized him because she had seen his image adorning one of the walls of Enki's orbiting space platform. Lord Astarte was wearing a long green and gold cape about his large reptilian frame—its color being quite similar to his own shimmering, scaly, horn-spotted skin. He looked at Lilith and then spoke.

"My dear child...a creation of Enki you must be," he said.

"Never have I laid eyes upon a creature of such grace and magnificence as yourself!" Lord Astarte appeared to become lost in Lilith's beauty as he stared at her. Shaking his head slightly, he snapped back into the moment. "Yes...by all means child, enter. My home is yours."

Astarte gestured toward the grand entranceway that slowly reticulated an opening from its center. Lilith smiled and stepped forward. Upon entering the great doorway, she walked down a long, mist-filled corridor that opened up to a great, tan marble hall accentuated by a number of waterfalls that came out of the walls, ponds and lush foliage everywhere. Lord Astarte emerged from around a tall marble column. Stately, graceful and immense, he walked toward Lilith with a calm and pleasant demeanor.

Lilith's eyes lit up when she saw the Anunaki Lord. She ran to him and embraced his large reptilian frame with a happiness and joy she could not contain. With wide eyes, Astarte pulled his head back and looked down at Lilith as he gently held her back at arm's length.

"Please, my dear...make yourself comfortable," he said as he gently motioned to a recessed area in the tan marble floor surrounded by eight thick, white marble columns. It was piled full of leather pillows and furs. Lilith smiled and nodded compliantly.

They walked over to the seating area, sat down and settled in. "And now my dear," he said, "you must tell me the tale of how you came to arrive at my door this day," Astarte said, as Lilith nestled herself at his feet. He gently curled his thick tail around her as she began the tale of her life and all the recent events that had ultimately brought her to his palace.

In the darkened shadows of the medical lab of Eridu, Enki watched Lilith and Astarte interact within a small surveillance monitor. Reaching out, he abruptly shut off the viewing dome... He was *not* pleased.

With a heavy sigh, he looked over at the medical bay across the room. On a small platform, the new human female that he and Ninmah had been working on had just risen from its tank and was now standing on the platform above the large glass vat of steamy dark water. Lit up by white light from below, gentle wisps of steam rose from her supple brown body.

Feeling somewhat intrigued by this new female, Enki raised an eyebrow as he gazed upon her finished form. This human female was a thicker, more voluptuous version of their original design with her larger breasts and fuller lips, butt and thighs. Enki got up from where he sat and walked over to her.

Looking straight ahead complacently, the new human female stood with her hands at her sides as Enki looked her over closely, touching her face lightly with his clawed fingertip.

"A truly magnificent creature you are," he said. "You will be known as...Eve."

Moving his large reptilian hand lightly over Eve's ample breasts and down her hip and thigh, she responds sensually to his touch and begins to caresses his arm as she touches herself softly. She moans and takes Enki by the hand as she begins to suck on his brownish-green scaled fingers. While looking at her, his eyes narrow.

"You will truly breed a fine race of humans."

Aroused by the human female's sensuality, Enki picks her up and carries her over to a nearby lab table. Standing there, he looks her over with hungry eyes and then proceeds to ravage her compliant body with a heated sexual intensity, lifting her long brown legs into the air as he mounts her again and again.

When he finally climaxes, Enki releases his seed deep into the voluptuous human female, and she in time, gives birth to his son. He would be named Cain—the Hybrid Son, firstborn child of Eve.

Chapter Eighteen

The skies are clear and the sun shines brightly over Astarte's grand ocean castle estate as Lilith sunbathes in one of the mansion's large pool areas. Looking out over the ocean waters, she lounges on a piece of furniture made of a dark metallic substance that looks more like a giant centipede than a reclining chair. With her long black hair pulled back, she wears a pair of black, cat-eye sunglasses, a black lizard skin bikini and black spiked heels. Her sleek, dark brown body is accentuated by the spiky black Rizqian jewelry that adorns her body from head to toe—curved, black talons through her ears; a black spiked collar around her neck; black horned bands around her arms, wrists, thighs and ankles; and spiny black jewelry on her fingers and toes. A small, dark wicker table with food, drinks and a variety of lotions sits next to her, and she has large sponge towels at her disposal stacked near the large swimming pool.

A very sleek and handsome tan-colored lizard man stood at attention nearby. He was poised as he watched over Lilith.

"Rancor," she called out, "would you be a dear and fetch me another Ambrosia salad."

"Yes, of course Magnificent One," he replied as he bowed his head softly.

Moments later, he returned carrying a curved, brown ceramic dish full of brightly colored fruits.

She smiled as she looked up at him. "Thank you Rancor," Lilith said. "Actually...I would like to thank you *and* your brothers for *all* the gracious hospitality that has been shown to me these past months."

Lilith sat up and pushed her sunglasses back. With wide eyes, she looked up at him.

"Upon my visits to the nearby estates of your brothers, I am *astounded* by the many wonders I have witnessed. The beautiful gardens created by Lord Bes, are absolutely amazing! His knowledge of botanical science is truly unsurpassed." She stared off into the distance. "I went to visit Lord Gestin and Enki's daughter Ninkas recently and beheld the unique vineyards that they have created...their wines are *magnificent*. And Lord Tammuz and Lady Inanna's vast fields of harvestable food plants are so bountiful and *so* delicious...absolutely amazing!"

"Most of all, I'm especially grateful for the use of the science laboratories of Lord Astarte!" She paused...frowning for a moment as she looked away. "The luxuries of your many sciences being so *previously* denied to me by our brother and my creator, Lord Enki"—she looked back up at him—"I am truly grateful to you all."

Rancor kneeled to address Lilith at eye level. "I'm sure that I speak for the rest of my brothers, as well as myself, when I tell you..." He gently reached out to remove her sunglasses from her forehead and put them on the side table.

"We have never experienced one as graceful and sensually magnificent as yourself." He took her by the hand as he looked into her eyes. "We are quite pleased to share with you what is truly yours, Gracious One."

He bowed his head when he told her, "My brethren and I are truly taken by your beauty and intellect." He looked back up at her with the utmost of sincerity.

"A *magnificent* example of Rizqian engineering...! You are truly without peer." With a sweep of his hand, he motioned toward the large palace. "Tonight, my fellow Elohim brothers and sisters will gather, and we will be celebrating the glory of your magnificence."

Lilith shaded her eyes with her arm as she looked up at Rancor.

"I am pleased as well." She sat up to touch him on the knee as she looked back at him with a genuine sincerity of her own.

"Your brothers have been most gracious. I am certain that the houses of Astarte, Tammuz, Ninkasi and Ama-arhus, will forever be in my heart."

Rancor gave her a puzzled look, for he did not fully grasp the affairs of the human heart. He stood up, closed his eyes and bowed his head softly toward her. Lilith laid back on her chair, smiling to herself as she stared out over the ocean waters.

As she lounged there peacefully, her mind wanders off and she is drawn to reflecting on her first Anunaki lover, Lord Enki. Enjoyable flashbacks of her times spent with him entered her mind as she relives the time they had spent aboard his space station above the earth and of the passion that they had shared. Suddenly, a disturbing image flashes in her mind. It was a vision of Enki having sex with *another* human female. The image startles her, and she shakes her head to clear it away.

The thought of being replaced as Lord Enki's lover by another human female gave Lilith a hollow feeling in her stomach. Her eyes begin to well up with tears as she looked at the ground, embraced in sad confusion. The sense of contentment she had felt was no longer present...for it had now been replaced by a feeling of great emptiness in her heart.

Many Anunaki had shown up for the celebration in Lilith's honor that evening and it was indeed, a *grand* success. An abundance of elaborately cut and arranged fruits and pastries filled the tables that lined Astarte's large ceremonial hall. The howling tones of the music that filled the palace hall were generated by a device situated among the rocks of one of the hall's many natural water features. Lit from below, it consisted of a series of crystal tubes that protruded from the rocks with water running through them. As they were stimulated, the varying fluid levels changed the wondrous tones of the music it was creating.

Lilith mingled among Lord Astarte's guests wearing nothing but a horned headdress and strands of small black shells around her waist, wrists and ankles that rustled softly as she walked.

The Anunaki drank much wine and smoked aromatic cannabis while Lilith belly danced for their enjoyment. At times throughout the evening, she would sit and watch her Anunaki hosts interact amongst themselves. She admired their boisterous pride as they shared their most recent achievements with one another.

Lilith raises her head as Lord Astarte beckons her to join them. "Lilith, my dear, will you dance for us again?" She smiles as she gets up, initiating her dance as her response.

Enjoying her sensual movements, Astarte's guests are completely in awe of her mannerisms. As she weaves in and out among them, Lilith has the Anunaki caught in the magic of her dance and they become mesmerized as they watch her. As she dances, the howling tones and the beat of the music begin to build faster and faster—working Lilith into a frenzy as her movements intensify with the increasing tempo. The Elohim are in awe, completely entranced as Lilith shakes her hips wildly with the crescendo of the loud music. When it peaks... she collapses into a heap on the floor.

There is a strange moment of silence as all who are gathered around slowly recover from the intensity of what they had just witnessed. The applause that begins slowly turns into a loud clamor of shouts and praise. Through Lilith, the Anunaki have felt a sensation that they are wholly unfamiliar with... and they are enamored by it.

After the performance, there is much rejoicing in Lilith's honor. They all wanted to get close to her to bask in the essence of her sensuality. There are many toasts made in her honor, as the festivities that evening continue on, late into the night.

✦ ✦ ✦

Moonbeams softly illuminated Astarte's grand hall through large open windows, while the sheer fabric that hung from them gently rustled in the warm ocean breeze.

Lilith, wearing a scant and sexy sky blue outfit made of a sheer draped fabric, tiptoed silently around the haphazardly scattered group of large, sleeping lizard men—Astarte, his court and all the other Anunaki who were strewn about the white marble palace floor. They slept where they had collapsed haphazardly after a very hedonistic celebration in Lilith's honor. One of them still had a drink in his hand that was half spilled onto the floor.

After quietly changing into an outfit that was more suited for travel, she packs a small rucksack with some food and supplies.

Lilith didn't want to leave, but in her heart, she knew that it was what she must do. Slowly, she turned to look back at the group as they slept and whispered, "Thank you...for all that you have shared."

In the dim light of the moon, Lilith tiptoed down the long, mist-filled, marble hallway and made her way toward the palace entrance. When she got there, she silently slipped out the large reticulated doorway and made her way north, down the dark, narrow dirt trail that ran along the rocky cliff line.

Chapter Nineteen

Unbeknownst to Lilith, her quiet departure under the cover of night had been witnessed by Lord Enki. From his personal office, he had been watching her every move within the crystal dome on his desk.

Angrily, Enki shut off the monitor and pushed an orange crystal panel on his computer console. He could not understand how Lilith had survived, much less found her way to Astarte's palace.

"Lucifer!" he snapped. "See me in my quarters at once."

Moments later, Lucifer entered his office. Enki was standing with his hands on his desk, holding his head down, consumed in thought.

He sighed deeply then looked up at his Captain of the Guard. "Lucifer," he said, "are you not truly my closest of brothers?"

The large golden lizard man nodded. "My lord."

"I am troubled . . . and I require your assistance." He glanced over at him. "The creature Lilith is still alive." He wheeled around and addressed Lucifer with a fiery, almost accusatory look in his eyes. "She has somehow survived the hardships of the desert and has been visiting the garden estates of our brethren." He calmed himself and stared blankly at the floor.

"Somehow, she has traveled to Lady Ama-arhus and Lord Abu's magnificent gardens," he said, softly shaking his head in disbelief.

Lucifer said nothing.

"She has spent time in the vineyards of Lord Gestin and my

He shook his head in disdain and looked

daughter Ninkasi and drank of their wines. And, she has also been to the vast fields of Lord Tammuz and Lady Inanna and tasted the bounty of their harvests." He shook his head in disdain and looked over at him.

"These hosts have shared with her the technologies of our gardens and our sciences. As of late," he said, his tone rising, "the house of Lord Astarte has been training her in the higher dynamics of the metaphysical arts!"

Lucifer could see Enki's rage growing.

"She is *my* creation! They had no authority!" Calming himself, he looked away. "They, of course, did have the free will to do as they pleased," he added, sounding as if he was trying to convince himself of this fact. "And *now* she's headed toward Edin."

Enki turned back to Lucifer and put his hand on his shoulder. His eyes were intense. "Her banishment is crucial now more than ever. This human female is wicked and filled with hate. She is a serious threat!" He gestured to the holographic images of the new human female image within the nearby computer monitors. "I am preparing to present the male human with his new bride, and Lilith must not be given the opportunity to destroy my creations with the fury of her newfound prowess."

He removed his hand from the captain's shoulder and spoke to him with authority. "You will guard the estate of Edin to ensure the safety of our new workforce."

Lucifer bowed his head. "Yes, my lord... your will be done."

Later, in the garden forest, a naked Eve followed Enki down a lush jungle path. The path opened up to a clearing and they approached a small, grass-roofed kiosk. Enki touched a small panel inside of the structure, activating the horn that would summon Adamu.

TOOKIE—TOOKIE—TOOKIE!

From behind the leaves of the trees, on a high branch, he soon appeared. Standing with his nose in the air, he looked down at

Enki and Eve, his muscular brown body glistening in the sunlight.

The arrogance in his face quickly turned to curiosity as he gazed upon his voluptuous new bride. He jumped down from the tree and slowly walked toward the two of them apprehensively. Standing before Enki, the stately lizard man reached out and put his large hand on Adamu's shoulder.

"Adamu my son," Enki said. He then put his hand behind Eve's back and gently nudged her toward Adamu. "This is Eve...she is to be your new bride."

Adamu looked at Eve in fascination and wonder as he touched her face with his fingertips. His face lit up as he beamed with excitement.

"Thank you, my lord. Your new creation is very beautiful, and I am honored to accept her as my new bride."

Enki bowed his head gently as he curled his large tan and green tail around his clawed feet. Adamu smiled as he took Eve by the hand. She smiled too and giggled as they ran off together down the jungle path.

Chapter Twenty

It was midday at Edin's southern security post. The small outpost was a pointed, earth-tone domed hut that was rough in texture and had the physical aesthetic of a large, unopened flower pod with a series of what looked like roots at its base that extended off into the ground in all directions. Overall, the small structure looked very natural in its bizarre, alien rain forest surroundings.

Inside the modest, dimly lit outpost, Lucifer wore a black cloak around his broad, golden scaled shoulders, as he reclined comfortably in a chair next to a crystalline computer console and monitor. The room's walls were bare, except for a large curved, dual blade, ceremonial sword displayed prominently on the softly lit wall behind him—the weapon's smaller blade being positioned just below the larger one at the hilt.

Inside of the crystalline security monitor, a yellow, holographic topography of the surrounding landscape turned slowly. Lucifer would glance at the screen occasionally, but he was more interested in the small computer monitor he was holding. It contained pointers and discipline exercises in the physical and metaphysical arts.

Suddenly, an alert went off.

Lucifer looked up from the small device and got up quickly to examine the monitor. Touching a small green crystal panel, he adjusted the screen. His eyes widened when the holographic image of Lilith came into focus.

Turning off the monitor, he stepped over to the sword on the wall and removed it. Weighing the ancient weapon in his hand, he could feel its powerful energy gently surge through him. Turning, he made his way toward the module's small doorway, prepared to confront Enki's creation, sword at the ready.

✦ ✦ ✦

As Lilith pushed a large palm frond that hung down in the middle of her path to the side, the dark, lush jungle trail that she had been traveling along opened up to a large, brightly lit clearing with the southern entranceway of Edin standing prominently before her.

The massive, dark metallic gateway loomed in front of her as it penetrated the curved force field of orange fire that surrounded the large Anunaki estate. Its immense, round doorway looked very much like a giant, curled up pill bug with thick horns that tapered down from its sides. Sleek, organic and alien in design, the gated force field was a sharp contrast to the rich green jungle that it stood next to.

As Lilith approached the large gateway, its doorway slowly began to open from its center. Without hesitation, she approached it eagerly.

The reticulated gateway opened and Lucifer stood there poised in the center of its entrance with his dual-bladed sword in his hand, the golden scales of his large, well-defined, sleek muscular body glistening in the midday sunlight. The long, fine horns on his head tapered back softly and looked like well-manicured dreadlocks, as the black cloak he wore draped behind his shoulders rustled gently in the afternoon breeze.

Lucifer's golden cream tail curled casually about his clawed feet as he looked down at Lilith with narrowed eyes.

Softly biting her lower lip, Lilith stepped back when she saw Lucifer, quite taken by his handsome appearance. Absently, she put her hand to her mouth and smiled a broad grin as she looked at him with approving eyes.

"I do not believe I've met this one who guards the palace grounds of Edin so diligently. You are *truly* a beautiful sight to behold," she said coyly.

"I am Lucifer, Captain of the Guard," he said proudly as he looked her over. "And *you* must be the disrespectful creation of my brother, who left this place with hate in her heart," he replied coldly and emotionlessly.

Lilith's jaw dropped as she put her hand to her chest in shock. Stepping forward to emphasize her point, she looked deep into Lucifer's dark reptilian eyes. Her eyes welled with tears.

"This is simply...not so," she said sadly, wiping away tears. "I am just like yourself and our brother Enki. I would *never* harm any of the creations in this garden." She stepped away and turned toward the gardens. She looked back at Lucifer. "Although I had come to see Lord Enki in an attempt to reclaim our love...if he will still not have me, I seek only to observe the plant and animal life here and reflect upon their many wondrous secrets."

Lucifer looked Lilith up and down. "Yes...I know who you are. But I must say...," he said softly, "you are not what I was expecting. Lord Enki has made you out to be some kind of hideous beast. And this is certainly not the case." He paused as he contemplatively stroked his chin whiskers.

"Personally, I find you to be quite *magnificent* in your grace and beauty. And I do sense truth in your heart," he said. "I have decided ...to let you pass."

Lilith's face lit up as she stepped forward and reached out to touch Lucifer on the arm. Gently pulling him down to her level, she gave him a soft kiss on the cheek.

"Thank you, beautiful one," she said.

Looking over her shoulder, she smiled at what awaited her inside Edin's garden estate. Excited, she turned from him and began to enter. Lucifer stared at the ground, lost in the moment, still taken by Lilith's kiss. Once he had regained his composure, he looked up and reached out to her.

"Lilith, wait," he said as he walked over to her. He got down on one knee as he took her by the hand and looked deep into her eyes.

"Before you leave... I have a gift for you."

Moved by his gesture, she held his hand and smiled softly.

"It has been through the discipline of many years of training, that I have mastered the harmony of the Celestial Spheres and Light," he said, as he closed his eyes. He opened them slowly, and then gestured skyward with a sweep of his arm. "In this, I have obtained dominion over the very stars that illuminate our night sky."

From his shoulders, Lucifer gently removed the soft, black cloak that he was wearing, draped it over his arm and presented it to her. "And so, I do give to you this garment of night, my dearest sister, upon which is sewn the moon and stars and all that appears in the night sky."

He stood and held it up before her. The back of the black velvet cloak displayed the swirl of the Milky Way galaxy, made of thousands of tiny diamonds sewn into its fabric. As he placed it on Lilith's shoulders, her eyes widened as she beamed with excitement.

"Wear this cloak and rule the Night, as I now rule the Day," he instructed.

Lilith shuddered from the rush of energy she got as the large black and silver cloak settled upon her shoulders. Every hair on her body began to stand on end. She glanced over at Lucifer with an excited wonder in her eyes while he looked at her knowingly, softly closing his eyes and nodding his reassurance to her.

Lilith's brown skin began to glow electric blue as she held out her arms in front of her in awe. The blue aura of her body began to glow brighter and brighter, as her hair turned from black to a charged electric silver, and her eyes began to softly glow the color of the moon. Suddenly, she gently lifted off the ground and slowly rose up into the air.

"Oh Lucifer!" she said, excitedly. "I *do* love this amazing gift. It is truly an amazing power to behold! I do love it...as much as I now love its dear, sweet giver!"

She gently floated over to Lucifer so she could be closer to him. With a serious look on her face, she said, "I have decided not to trouble our brother here in the gardens today. Instead, I will travel to the fertile lands far to the east of here and raise up a wondrous garden estate of *my own*." She looked at him with a coy allure then reached out and put a hand on his broad shoulder.

"Perhaps...you will come to visit me there, my love?" she asked him as she gently touched his handsome reptilian face and smiled. "Lucifer, my Beautiful One. You shall one day come to my garden. Come—and I will share with you its many splendors."

Lucifer bowed his head as she smiled at him and gently turned away. He watched Lilith as she spread the black and silver Cloak of Night and rose up into the air, floating off into the blue afternoon sky toward the Eastern lands.

Chapter Twenty-one

Lilith's estate of D'hainu's was a spectacular garden paradise. Surrounded by lush rainforest jungles, and accentuated by many glistening waterfalls, three great rivers made up its outermost boundaries. In the bright afternoon sun, Lilith was working in her lush botanical gardens, smiling to herself as she picked dry leaves from some of the ponytail palm ferns. Her grand estate was filled with a great variety of indigenous Earth plant life—trees and bushes, flowers and herbs, grasses, vines, ferns and mosses.

On the hillside behind her… nestled between the crest of two mountains, sat her grandiose palace home. The majestic castle blended in perfectly with its garden environment in that it looked very much like an arrangement of large glass flowers sticking out of an enormous tree stump.

The flowers of the palace roof consisted of massive, flower petal-shaped glass windows of many colors. A network of intricately curved, green metallic beams that formed the vine, stem and flower petal structures supported the large glass panels. The bottom part of the palace looked like a tree stump with roots at its base that bent off in many directions, as a variety of random window holes and doorway entrances spotted its rough bark like surface.

In the light of the early morning sun, Lilith hummed a little tune to herself as she made her rounds through her vibrant botanical garden estate. Along the trail, she stopped and gently reached her hand out toward a group of plants—and they responded to her. The plants of the jungle would often turn toward Lilith, moving with intelligence and affection as they softly interacted with her. She smiled back to them, her body language expressing a true joy—the heartfelt joy of being among friends. Going over to one of the ferns, Lilith leaned over, cupped her hand to her mouth and whispered to it. The fern recoiled slightly, but after a moment, it submitted and offered one of its branches to her. She took a cutting from it and put it in the pocket of a small apron she wore around her waist.

After Lilith had said goodbye to her garden friends, she turned toward home and began her walk back to the palace.

When Lilith reached her magnificent home, she went to the far side of the building to where her greenhouse laboratory was located. Its large roof resembled giant flowers like the rest of the building, but was made of clear glass panels instead of colored ones. The inside of the structure housed an enormous, breathtaking, living rain forest. When she reached the conservatories entrance, she went inside through a small round doorway in the base of the giant tree stump.

Once inside the vast rainforest arboretum, the sweet scent of dank vegetation, orchids, gardenia and jasmine engulf her senses as the sounds of running water and the loud screeching of wild birds and monkeys fill her ears. She walks the narrow path, along streams and past waterfalls, through the many exotic plants that fill the huge, multilevel conservatory on her way to its botanical laboratory.

Surrounded by the thick jungle of her immense greenhouse, the brightly lit laboratory is constructed of glass and stainless steel. Inside, racks of glass test tubes line the walls, as rows and rows of hydroponically grown plants fill up most of the room.

Removing the plant cuttings from her small apron, Lilith puts them on one of the laboratory tables, and then takes the small test tubes and places two to three cuttings from the different plants into them, filling them with either a blue, red, or orange fluid after-wards. She then places the different tubes in stainless steel racks that she has lined up in rows on the laboratory table.

With all of her cuttings situated, Lilith was done with her business and left the botanical science lab to walk through the vast arboretum and check on the other plants. The screeching cries of monkeys and exotic birds fill the lush green habitat as she walks through the rows of various rare and unique plant life planted in the long, curved racks that run throughout the enormous arboretum. Along the way, she inspected the various plants along the path that she has been cultivating to see how they are faring, making notations on a small chart she carried with her.

The many unique crossbred plants were growing healthy and full. Some of them were even taking over areas with their extended over growth. As she pruned them back, Lilith smiled, being very pleased with how healthy they had become.

When she was done working in her greenhouse, Lilith left and went into the palace. Inside, delicate, aromatic Acacia wood trim accentuated the high arched ceilings, smooth curved walls and hallways. Her reception hall was open and spacious, with a large, natural waterfall and Koi pond feature located in its center, all connected to an upper terrace. Lush palms and ferns adorned the central hall and were planted in many spots throughout the palace.

Lilith had also incorporated large, saltwater fish tanks into the walls of the palace's main hallways that contained many types and varieties of colorful sea life and sea creatures. Sometimes she would literally spend hours in her hallways watching the sea life interact. At the moment, Lilith was on her way to her kitchen where she had been preparing baked goods earlier that day.

The palace kitchen was in essence, a witch's dream kitchen, complete with amethyst crystal countertops, modern appliances and a heated stone slab that was currently cooking a large cauldron of vegetable stew. As Lilith approached the spacious, sunlight filled room, the pleasant aromas of pastry and the spice of stew filled her senses. Her large, black house cat, Mooracus rubbed on her leg, eagerly awaiting an afternoon snack. She reached down and pet him on his head and down his back.

"Are you hungry, Mooracus? Mommy has some tasty treats for you!"

She broke him off a piece of dried meat that she had hanging on a rack next to some herbs that she had recently picked. Going over to her oven, she pulled out the large potpie that had been baking and put it on a stone countertop, where she waited for it to cool.

One morning, after taking a stroll through the aquarium-filled halls within her palace, Lilith began to climb the large, spiral staircase that went up to the lofty, glass flower ceiling. High above, a small platform that allowed her to look out over D'hainu's lush garden estate sat nestled among the thick, green metal beams that made up the supportive stem network holding the magnificent ceiling aloft. Here she would come to take in the spectacular view and meditate on her energy.

As Lilith sat and focused on her center, she reflected on how much she had achieved in two years. The sense of accomplishment was a most gratifying feeling and her body began to glow with a gentle green light that radiated from within as she became more and more empowered by the gentle energies that ran through everything around her. It had been through awakening to these webs of power, and then spinning them into whatever she desired, that she had achieved most everything she had created in D'hainu.

When she was finished with her meditation, Lilith went back down stairs and walked over to a small altar within her main hall, where a very special, ornate wooden flute that she had handcrafted was on display. She took the instrument from its stand and left the palace through its large front entranceway.

The afternoon sun lights up the plants of jungle a bright vibrant green as Lilith walks down a trail to one of her favorite magical places. Next to a waterfall on one of the many small streams that wound through her estate, she sits down among the trees and begins to play a beautiful melody on her special flute. The sweet tones of her music add an even more enchanting quality to her gardens as they float through the air, echoing softly throughout the land.

Playing songs that are a natural expression of her spirit, she attracts the attention of many creatures within the forest. Slowly, they gather around her in a curiously enchanted manner. The birds in the trees pipe in... mimicking and harmonizing Lilith's tones. Together they create beautiful melodies, long into the afternoon.

✦ ✦ ✦

A couple of days later, Lilith returns to her greenhouse laboratory to check on the new hybrid experiments. She is very excited to see how well the splicing had gone. When she gets there, she finds that some of her crossbred plants have shriveled and died or simply not fused, and that some of them have successfully combined, to make strange healthy new plants.

Lilith looked at the dead cuttings sadly, but smiles and feels a great sense of achievement when she examines her healthy new crossbreeds. With the hopes of reproducing the fruit she had known and loved in Edin, she takes the group of healthy plants and transplants them into large hydroponic pots in racks that are closer to the ground. As Lilith removes the root balls from their old containers, she speaks softly and hums a gentle tune to the small plants. When she is finished with her work, Lilith blows the baby plants tender kisses.

"Goodbye, my dear children... may you all grow up to be healthy and strong." she tells them as she leaves for the day.

Early one morning, many weeks later, Lilith returned once again to her greenhouse laboratory. To her pleasant surprise, almost all of the crossbred plants had grown into bushes and small trees; each type of plant having a different type of colorful fruit hanging from it. She was very happy as she checked on their ripeness. Taking some of the more mature produce over to a small oval, stainless steel countertop, she cut slices from each one and then sampled a bite from each.

Lilith was not pleased with the first fruit's flavor... it was *awful*. With a look of disgust, she spit out the nasty tasting piece of fruit and took a bite of different slice. She winced at its bitterness.

The other slices offered no better results and Lilith clenched her fists in frustration, as she looked at the floor, disappointed and angry. Raising her head, she let out a disturbing cry of anguish.

"AAAAAAaaaaaaahhhhhH!"

She raised her clenched fists to the sky and cried out, "Enki! Why have you forsaken me?" She sobbed. "Why have you denied me the fruits of your gardens? I long to taste the sweet nectar of cantaloupe and strawberries! *How* can I be expected to set my tables without them?"

Lilith managed to calm herself, but was still very upset. She stormed out of her laboratory and walked through her palace in a fluster, fuming and extremely frustrated. She had now concluded that if she could not reproduce these off-world plants on her own, she would simply have to obtain them from within the gardens of Edin. She was still very upset as she went through the palace closing windows and doors. It was after she had fed her fish and cat, that she grabbed the black cloak that Lucifer had given her, and went outside to put it on.

As soon as Lilith put the heavy, black fabric around her shoulders, her skin began to glow electric blue, her hair turned white and she slowly began to rise up into the air. She then rose quickly into the sky and flew westward toward the Anunaki's garden of Edin. Lilith would have the fruits she had become accustomed to, one way or another.

Passing over forests and rivers, Lilith flew swiftly toward the Edin. When she finally reached the force field of fire that surrounded its estate, she located the massive gate at the Southern Entryway and gently set down in front of it.

It wasn't long before the round, reticulated doorway opened and there stood Lucifer, lowered sword in hand. With a subtle gleam in his eye, he smiled at her gently.

"So..." he said softly, "I see that you have returned to Edin, Magnificent One."

Lilith bowed her head. "Yes, Lucifer, I have returned." She looked up at him as she slightly cocked her head to the side. "My beloved...I am wondering. *Why* are you still standing guard here at the Southern Gates? Have you become Lord Enki's servant?" she asked coyly.

"I assure you, I have become *no one's* servant, my love," Lucifer replied. "I am here as a favor to Lord Enki, whom I care for as a brother. He tells me that I am to watch for She Who Has Been Cast Out. Enki tells me that her soul is small and dark, and filled with the spirit of evil."

He stood there, looking past her into the distance. "In this, she would not be able to stand comfortably in the presence of the light of my being."

Lilith grew saddened at his statement but quickly wiped away the tears that came to her eyes. "Lucifer, my beloved, I am certainly not she. I stand content in your light and share it as my own."

Lucifer looked at her shrewdly, thinking to himself, and then gave her his personal stance on the matter. "I have looked deep into your heart my dear, and I can easily sense that you bear no malice." His demeanor softened as he looked into her eyes. "You have already proven this to me." He became poised and serious.

"I have given you my heart, my trust and my power." He bowed his head. "You have, in return, offered allegiance, graciousness and respect." He looked at her softly. "These are traits that I honor and value greatly."

He stepped over to Lilith and knelt down on one knee. The massive sword he carried with him in his left hand supported his upper body weight as he leaned on it casually. "Well then, dear sweet Lilith, tell me...what *have* you been doing with yourself? And why have you come to Enki's gardens this day?"

Lilith put her hand on his arm. "Oh Lucifer, I have used your gifts well!" Her eyes lit up with excitement as she gestured eastward. "The lands to the east have provided me a rich and fertile forest to maintain a magnificent garden and build a beautiful home, complete with a botanical laboratory that Enki *himself* would be proud to call his own." She folded her arms and nodded her head to emphasize the fact, "I call it D'hainu." She looked at Lucifer and reached out to him, putting her hand on his arm.

"Although I have managed to create a variety of wondrous cross-pollinated hybrid vegetation in my laboratories, with many strange fruit and flower essentials," she continued, looking deep into Lucifer's dark reptilian eyes. "I have one problem, my love," she said as she turned away and looked at the floor. "Although the variety in my garden is great, I have only the fruit of this world to work with. I have tried many times to reproduce the fruits and herbs of your gardens' otherworldly plant life and have encountered many unfavorable results."

She wheeled around and confronted Lucifer with her frustrating dilemma.

"With all this wondrous power... I cannot reproduce the genetics of these otherworldly botanicals that you and your brethren have brought and planted here in Edin's gardens." She turned from him and looked out over the alien plant life inside the Estate. "I must visit your gardens," she said. Turning back around, she confided in him. "I will only take a few small cuttings and some seeds from the off-world plants here, so that they can be planted in *my* garden... that I may enjoy them and the fruits that they bear." She paused as she looked at Edin's interior. "We, of course, will not want to disturb our brother Lord Enki." She looked at him. "My love, allow me to enter, and I will assure you discretion."

Lucifer bowed gracefully and motioned toward the gardens. "I am fully confident in your abilities Lilith," he said softly. "Enter and take what samples you need." He stepped forward and took her by the hand as he looked deeply into her eyes.

"You have captured my heart, Magnificent One, and there is very little that I would deny you."

Lilith smiled as she gently pulled Lucifer down to reach his face and kissed him on the cheek.

"Thank you again, Beautiful One," she whispered. Lowering her eyes, she then turned from him and slipped off into the lush green, alien garden.

Once she was inside Edin's gardens, Lilith snuck over to a dense group of strange-looking trees and took off her Cape of Night. Folding it carefully, she hid the precious garment in a secluded area within the small thicket and then left the cluster of trees carefully to slink off into the jungle garden's thick, rainforest interior.

She knew she would need to conceal herself immediately, so as soon as she started walking…Lilith began to metamorphous, transforming her body into that of a large snake. Upon her transformation, she was now a twelve-foot-long, tan and black boa constrictor with a cream-colored underbelly.

Lilith slithered off into the bushes, considerably much less detectable to the small Anunaki security lenses that were placed discriminately all throughout the interior of Edin's estate.

Throughout the day, Lilith moved through the large rain forest jungle collecting plant cuttings and seed pods from the bizarre, alien flora. There were so many different types of strange bushes and trees and flowers found only in Edin's gardens and nowhere else. The range of biodiversity was quite vast, with some of the plants having, fuzzy leaves of purple, green and pink blossoms with slender curled offshoots coming off them, while others had bright, blue, orange or yellow colored fruits and flowers of the oddest shapes and sizes. Carrying the various strange cuttings and seedpods she would gather in her snake mouth, she would routinely place the clones in a carpet of damp moss next to her collected seeds and hide them under random bushes throughout the lands.

While she was moving through the grasses, almost done with her seed and clone gathering mission, Lilith happened upon someone quite suddenly . . .

It was Eve.

Chapter Twenty-two

Lilith watched from behind the jungle grasses as Eve went about her duties manicuring and harvesting the estate's garden. She admired her meticulous nature and was pleased to know that her replacement was caring for the gardens with such a devoted finesse. Rearing up on her hind end and transforming back into her human form, she stepped out of the thick, green jungle from behind a large palm frond.

As Lilith approached Eve, she startled her. Stopping what she was doing, Eve stepped back, uncertain of what to make of the mysterious stranger who looked much like herself. Lilith tried to reach out to her but slowly withdrew her hand and placed it over the center of her chest.

"I am Lilith," she told her. "I am very much like a *sister* to you. Do you understand...? Sister."

"I... think I understand," Eve said softly. "I am Eve." She looked Lilith up and down in fascinated wonder. "You are like me, aren't you?"

Lilith smiled and nodded. "Yes, that's right!"

"Then you must know Lord Enki, my father and creator." She paused. "Did he create you as well?"

"Yes, I too am a daughter of Lord Enki and I have come to know him *very* well." Lilith's thoughts shifted, she looked down at the ground in dismay and then stared off into the dark green jungle.

"It saddens me…but I have not spoken to Lord Enki in quite some time."

"That's all right," Eve smiled and said, "We can visit him now." She took Lilith by the hand to try to get her to come with her, but Lilith would not move. She softly pulled her hand away from Eve's grasp.

"No, sister…I cannot follow you to see Enki." She looked away and sighed heavily. "All that I can tell you is that it would hurt my heart too much to see him right now." Putting her hand on Eve's shoulder, she looked her in the eye with great seriousness. "I would rather Lord Enki did *not* know of my presence here today."

Eve's eyes narrowed. "I think I understand," she said slowly, "and I will respect your wishes." She looked back at Lilith and changed the subject. "So if you're not here to visit Lord Enki, why *are* you here?"

Lilith motions for Eve to join her on the ground next to a fallen tree and Eve sits down on the grass, making herself comfortable as she leans back against the small log. Being completely captivated, Eve is in awe as Lilith tells her story.

"For reasons too hurtful to discuss, I was relieved of my duties here in Edin, and I left to pursue my own endeavors." She paused as she stared off—reflecting on what she'd been through. "It wasn't easy…but in time, I made new acquaintances. And I've learned from what they had to share with me." She looked back at Eve.

"My roads have been well traveled…and I have learned *much* from my many gracious hosts." Lilith smiled at Eve with a proud excitement. "I have even created a wondrous garden palace estate of my own in the lands far to the east of here!"

Eve's face lit up.

"My gardens are *very* beautiful," Lilith continued, then a look of sadness appeared on her face. "But I do often long for the company of the many wondrous plants and flowers here in these gardens that are not of this world and grow only here in Edin." She looked up at Eve. "Enki and his brethren, the Anunaki, have traveled the stars and they have brought much of the plant life here from their home world of Rizq. Most of the plant life in Edin can neither be found on this world nor reproduced."

Lilith paused to gauge whether or not Eve understood her, but she was completely enthralled, so she continued, "I am sampling the smallest of cuttings to produce clones for my garden, so that I too may share in the joy of their company and the harvest of their bounty!"

Eve sat up eagerly. "My sister... I love the plants here as well. That is my life here in Edin, taking care of plants every day, and I love it. They are like... friends."

Lilith nodded her understanding. "Oh yes, my dear, they are very much like friends." She softly reached out to a nearby vine that hung down from a tree branch above them. It responded gently and moved toward her hand and the two exchanged a gentle caress. Eve was amazed at what she was seeing.

"Sister...!" Eve exclaimed. "How have you awakened that plant? It comes to you as if it knows you!"

"Well, actually," Lilith explained, "this tree comes to me because I know *it*. I have been introduced to a special aspect of the world around us—*everything* is alive. Once I became awakened to this, I found friends where I never could have imagined."

"You say you were introduced to the world around you?" Eve asked with a puzzled look on her face. "By whom?"

Lilith smiled as she took note of Eve's childlike innocence.

"If you wait right here for just a moment," Lilith said cryptically, "I will return shortly." She stood up and slipped off into the bushes again. Once hidden, she morphed back into a large boa constrictor and slithered off to a nearby collection of seeds and cuttings that she had gathered. There, she took a large, partially developed, red mushroom with a white stalk into her mouth.

Carrying the mushroom, she made her way back to where Eve was waiting for her. She returned to her human form just before she got back to the small jungle clearing and emerged with her hand hidden behind her back. She walked over to where Eve was patiently waiting for her and knelt down. From behind her back, Lilith gently presented the Amanita Muscaria. As she held the unopened mushroom out in front of her by its thick, white stalk, it looked very much like a big, red apple.

"This is Aman," Lilith said softly. "The Way-Shower—the gracious host that has awakened my mind and shown me the true nature of our universe."

Eve's eyes lit up as she put her hand to her mouth apprehensively. She pointed at the mushroom.

"I recognize this plant, sister," she exclaimed. "It is from Lord Enki's sacred gardens. These plants are *forbidden* to partake of!"

Lilith looked deeply into Eve's eyes. "Yes... I was told the very same thing," she explained softly. "But these magical plants beckoned me to partake of them, and I did... I regret nothing." She paused for a moment then continued. "This magical mushroom has opened my eyes to what my connection to the world *actually* is—an inner connection that I was not aware of in my prior state." She looked up at the sky with wide eyes. "The world around me became so much more vivid and alive. I am *part* of it, and it is part of me."

Eve looked down in confusion and held her head in her hands. After a moment, she looked up and stared at Lilith with tears in her eyes.

"I *do* desire to respect the wishes of my beloved creator, but when I gaze upon you, and I think of what you have become... I feel as if I am a lesser being." She teared up even more. "Please Lilith, my dear sweet sister; please introduce me to this magical aspect of the world that you have come to recognize. Introduce me to Aman," she pled, "and I will partake of its flesh."

Eve continued to sob gently. Lilith closed her eyes for a moment and smiled knowingly. She broke off a piece of the mushroom and offered it to her. Eve wiped the tears from her eyes and cautiously reached out to take the piece of mushroom. After a moment, she put it into her mouth and slowly chewed, wincing at the flavor.

"Mnaah...! That tastes terrible, sister!" Eve said.

As Lilith ate some of the mushroom also, she winced at its taste as well. Getting up, she grabbed a large seedpod that was lying on the ground nearby and the pitcher of plant water that Eve had been using earlier. Breaking the pod open, she handed one of the halves to Eve and then filled them with water. With a look of disgust on her face, Eve eagerly drank long and deep.

Lilith took a long drink as well. "That may be true, but the taste will pass. Here...have some more water."

As the two drank the cool water together, they looked at each other and slowly, they began laughing at how awful the mushroom had tasted. After a moment, they manage to compose themselves and with a smile on her face, Lilith says to Eve, "Okay, let's get started."

She pats the ground as she beckons Eve to sit down on the ground in front of her. Eve does so compliantly and Lilith begins to gently rub her shoulders.

"Relaxation is the first step in awakening to the world around you. Breathe deeply and relax your shoulders," she tells her.

Eve takes a deep breath and lets her shoulders relax, as Lilith gently moves her into a reclined position. She has Eve roll onto her stomach and begins to give her a full body, deep tissue massage.

When she is done, Lilith stops and lightly sweeps her hand over the full length of Eve's body. Lilith then begins to touch Eve more lightly as she works with her energy on a much more subtle level. She starts to gently move her hands over Eve's entire body without actually touching her skin, and then... the mushrooms start to kick in.

Slowly, both women begin to hallucinate intensely. Lilith lies down in the grass next to Eve, who rolls over onto her side so they could lay face to face. At this point, both girls eyes were now fully dilated and looked like big, black saucers.

For Eve, the rich green jungle begins to gently breathe and the plants around them seem to glow softly as the rainforest comes alive. The plant life all around them slowly becomes kind of a pulsating, psychedelic paisley swirl.

When she looks over at Lilith, she notices that a green light has begun to glow from the center of her chest, while golden sparkles softly emanate from her eyes. Sitting up, Lilith reaches out to her to touch her face. Eve closes her eyes and moans softly; enjoying the soft sensuality of her touch as she gently nuzzles her hand.

"Mmmmmmmnnh," she murmurs softly.

Golden light was now emanating from Lilith's entire body as Eve sits up. Reaching out, Lilith embraces her as she guides her back into a reclined position. Touching Eve's mouth gently, she gives her a long, deep, passionate kiss.

As they lay there, kissing passionately in the jungle grass, the plant vines on the ground slowly begin to creep in and surround the two in a very gentle manner. The jungle vines move in slowly toward the couple and begin to form a heart-shaped enclosure around them. Within moments, the surrounding clusters of vines spontaneously begin to blossom and bloom into a full spectrum of colorful flowers.

With a smile, Lilith reaches over, plucks one of the red blossoms and places it between Eve's legs at her crotch. She giggles then reaches over and grabs an orange flower blossom and places it on Eve's belly, just below her navel, following it with a yellow blossom between her navel and chest. She follows up with a green flower in the center of her chest, a blue flower on her throat and a purple one above her eyes.

Eve lay on the ground peacefully for a few moments, but slowly loses her composure when she begins to giggle uncontrollably. Unable to stop laughing, she sits up and the flowers fall to her sides. She smiles at Lilith and touches her softly about the face and shoulders, as the two tenderly embrace each other for another long and passionate kiss.

The two girls lean back into the grass and touch each other's bodies with a heightened sense of arousal, as they explore one another. Lilith maneuvers her face down between Eve's legs and begins to pleasure her orally with an unrelenting intent. Eve's eyes widened, as Lilith skillfully tongues her moist nether regions.

The girls made love passionately for what could have easily been hours. It was afterwards, while resting peacefully in each other's arms and enjoying the serenity of the jungle gardens, when suddenly, an owl startled them with his hooting.

"WHOOO…WHOOO…WHOOO…"

They sat up quickly and looked around. The sound of someone approaching could be heard off in the distance.

Lilith looked at Eve, then back into the jungle.

"It's Adamu," she whispered. "He's looking for you."

Chapter Twenty-three

E ve merely giggled at what Lilith said and whispered, "If
Adamu's here...let's go get him!"

Lilith looked at her sharply. "Adamu and I were not on the best
of terms the last time we shared company," Lilith said, seriously,
while Eve tried not to laugh. "I have an idea though." She turned
to Eve and put her hand on her shoulder to make sure that she
had her full attention. "I will stay hidden while you speak with
Adamu," she instructed. "You will comfort him, but tell him that
you will not share your body with him until he eats these pieces of
mushroom that you will give him."

Eve looked perplexed but nodded her head in accordance with
Lilith's wishes as she took the pieces of mushroom from her.

"He'll want to know what it is...but do not tell him," Lilith said.
"He *will* submit, and when he does, the Way-Shower will begin to
awaken him. *Then* we will tell him of my presence here."

Eve looked at Lilith and bowed her head. She trusted her
judgment. Concealing the mushrooms in her hand, she got up and
made her way toward where Adamu was looking for her.

Eve emerged from behind the thick green foliage into a small
clearing along the jungle path. Smiling, she beckoned Adamu
by waving to him, giggling to herself as she tried to keep her
composure.

"I am here, my love!" she announced, trying not to laugh as she sat down on the ground.

Adamu was relieved as he followed Eve's voice to the clearing. Although he was happy that he had finally found his mate, when he looked at her, he noticed something slightly odd about her appearance.

"Eve! I've been looking all over for you. What have you been doing?"

Eve just smiled, giggled and looked up at him. She was in absolutely no condition to give him a comprehensive response. Patting the ground, she simply invited him to sit down next to her. He was a little confused, but Adamu did as she requested. Suddenly, without warning, Eve pounced on top of him. Grabbing him by the face, she gave him a long, deep, wet kiss on the mouth and the two rolled around on the grass playfully. Becoming aroused, Adamu made his advances to enter Eve's body, but she gently pulled away from him and smiled.

"No, my love, you may not have me in that way...until you partake of this substance." She showed him the mushrooms.

Adamu sat up and looked at the small pieces of mushroom. "What is it?" he asked, "and why are you acting so strangely?"

"It is food, my love," Eve said.

Adamu accepted the mushrooms pieces nonchalantly and put them in his mouth. He then made a disturbing face due to their terrible taste. Eve went over to a nearby tree, grabbed a dried gourd that hung from a branch and dipped it into a small water tank underneath the tree. She handed it to him and he took a long drink.

"Woman...! That food tasted awful! And your behavior is most peculiar! *What* is going on with you?"

Eve took a long, deep breath as she sat down. She looked up at Adamu and gestured that he sit as well, so he sat down next to her. Slowly, she got behind him and started to rub his shoulders and neck, softly nuzzling his ear with her face.

"I assure you that all is well, my love," she told him. "Just sit back and relax. I will comfort your body... You must be weary from your long day of toil." She moved her hands across Adamu's muscular brown body, her touch becoming more sensual as she caressed him gently and kissed his mouth and face. She kissed him on the neck and shoulders and slowly moved down his torso to his midsection, where she gently embraced his manhood with her mouth. Adamu leaned back against the forest lawn on his elbows as he rolled his eyes back in his head.

Adamu lay there as he enjoyed Eve's oral attentions. Her enhanced sense of arousal had caused her to become completely infatuated by his penis in that it looked very much like a magic mushroom to her. After much meticulous attention, Adamu sat up and took Eve by the arms. Pulling her up and looking into her eyes, he grabbed her around the waist and kissed her on the mouth as he laid her down onto her back. He mounted her with a raging passion and the two made love in a frenzied heat of sexual exploration, right there on the lush and beautiful jungle pathway.

It was during their lovemaking that a look of bewilderment suddenly crossed Adamu's face. There seemed to be something different about the jungle around him. He shook his head, blinking, then, shook it again.

"Did you see that?" he whispered.

Eve moans a sensual, incomprehensible response, "Mmnhahh..."

He decides not to pursue the question and refocuses his attention on the amazing sex he is having with his sensual new partner. He did feel a little strange, but he decides that it was a good strange. The two ultimately climax together in unison as they culminate their lovemaking with an explosive orgasm. Adamu closes his eyes as his body shudders with an energy that he could feel all the way from his head to his toes.

Rolling over onto his back, Adamu's mouth hung open as he breathed heavily, staring up at the jungle with wide, dilated eyes.

The rich, green canopy had begun to gently undulate, as the plants all seemed to come alive. The colors of the rain forest were more vivid as all its sounds became amplified.

He notices as the chirping of the birds and low buzz of the insects slowly becomes louder and louder.

"buuuuuzzzZZZZZZ...!"

A yellow bird flies by in slow motion across the gap in the breathing, green forest canopy. It leaves a trail of yellow tracers as it flies by. Lifting his right hand, he looks at it. His fingers also leave tracer trails as he slowly waves them in front of his face.

He lay there, staring up at the jungle "Eve...," he said, breathing heavily, "why does the forest...look...so...strange?" The jungle foliage continued to undulate, as if it were breathing.

Adamu sits up and looks over at Eve. Her brown skin now has a white luminescence glow about it as she sits up as well, and as she does, she leaves tracer trails where her body had once been.

Slowly, she turned and looked at him with wide, dilated eyes and with a grin, she said to him softly, "Welcome...to the real world!"

Adamu was uneasy and Eve moved closer to him, putting her hand on his shoulder.

"Do not be alarmed, my love," she said. "All is as it should be. You have merely been *awakened*."

"But how did—," he began.

"It was *Lilith* who—," she started to say.

"Lilith! You've seen her?" he asked. His eyes began to well up with tears. "We...used to be in love. I knew her as Lilitu then." He began to cry. "And I rejected her...I feel so terrible!" He paused as he struggled with his reflection on what had happened. "I was jealous...jealous of her prowess as a hunter, and I immediately took offense." He began to open up and cry even harder. "I thought she was mocking my abilities," he continued through sobbing sentences. "And then, I forced her to share her body with me...I forced her…and I took from her." He sobbed. "I made her weep from the pain I inflicted upon her."

Eve got up and put her arm around Adamu's shoulder to comfort him.

"Adamu, my love," she said. "Don't be sad… Although I may not know the extent of your sorrow, I can feel the truth in your words." She touched his face and got him to look her in the eye. "The person you should be telling this to is *Lilith*. Do not be alarmed…but she is here, with us!"

He looked up at her and regained his composure somewhat as he wiped away his tears.

At that moment, Lilith stepped out from behind a large group of giant palm fronds. She was radiant, her dark brown skin glowing with a soft green light. Looking at Adamu, she smiled softly. He was in awe as he gazed upon her radiance and he burst out sobbing again.

"Oh, Lilitu…," he wailed, "I loved you so much! And I am so sorry."

Lilith felt a sense of pity for Adamu and she walked over to him. Reaching out, she gently caressed his wet, teary-eyed face.

"Adamu," she said softly, "my dear sweet man. At one time, I thought of you an equal among the dogs. But I am Lilith now. I have a much greater understanding of the world since we last shared company." She looked deeply into his eyes. "I forgive you."

Adamu reached out for Lilith and she put her arms around him. He smiled and closed his eyes tightly as they held each other. After a long hug, the two pulled away from each other slowly. Adamu held Lilith at arm's length and looked her up and down. Eve came closer and stood next to them, smiling as she put her hand on the small of Lilith's back.

"You are Lilith now," Adamu said. "You have changed…I like it." He touched her face and lips then pulled her in closer with one arm and Eve with the other. A gentle grin came across his face. It felt good to be with both women. Happy in their resolve, he gave Lilith a deep kiss on the mouth as Eve held them both, smiling to herself as she watched their passionate reunion.

"I have *truly* missed your embrace Lilith," he whispered to her softly.

As Lilith and Adamu kiss tenderly, Eve gently caressed their muscular, brown bodies. The two of them slowly turn and look at her then back at each other, and they smile in unison. Reaching out to Eve, they gently guide her down onto the green, forest lawn and begin kissing and caressing her voluptuous, naked brown body.

As Adamu nuzzles Eve's large breasts, Lilith sits up and touches him gently about his shoulders. She hovers over them as Adamu sends Eve into a state of heated sexual arousal. Eve grabs Lilith from behind her waist and pulls her to her face, gently kissing her on the stomach and pelvis. Adamu repositions himself and mounts Eve while she passionately kisses and licks Lilith's well defined body.

The three make love with an unbridled sexual abandon, as they uninhibitedly explore each other's naked bodies. The small orgy continues on until the early evening until they all fall asleep, nestled hidden in their jungle love nest. The shadows in the jungle become long, as the final light of the setting sun begins to reach the horizon.

It is almost dark when Adamu awakens and finds he needs to relieve his bladder. Quietly, he removes himself from the dark recesses of the low hanging palm fronds where Eve and Lilith lie hidden, passed out in each other's arms, and walks over to the thick wall of jungle on the opposite side of the small clearing to urinate by some bushes.

As he is relieving himself, he notices that the dark, undulating shadows cast by the green foliage all around him have started to gently change and take on a menacing presence. Images of small, dark, evil little faces begin to appear in the empty shadows with fiery red eyes and dark, gaping, jagged mouths. As Adamu slowly begins to look all around him, the little faces are everywhere. A noise in the jungle startles him and something screams, while the buzz of insects begins to grow louder and louder.

"buuuuuuuuuzzzZZZZZZZ...!"

Somewhere in the distant jungle, a creature screams again, as it has just become someone's dinner.

Adamu is struck with fear and he lets out a terrified scream of his own.

"Aaaaaaaaaaaaaaahhhhhhhhh...!"

Chapter Twenty-four

The two women glance at each other, alarmed when they hear Adamu's scream. Sitting up quickly, Lilith tries to call out to him.

"Adamu!" she shouted in a hushed tone. "What are you doing? Get back here!"

She turned to Eve. "If he's not careful, he will alert security… and *that* would not be good."

Eve knew Lilith was serious when she saw the look on her face. "If Enki sees Adamu in the state that he's in, he will know something peculiar is happening in his gardens—and he will *not* be pleased."

Eve nodded as she agreed with her. They got up and started to run toward the direction where Adamu had disappeared into the dark, thick, jungle. Lilith then stopped for a moment, realizing that she had better conceal herself and metamorphose back into a boa constrictor. Transforming quickly, she caught up to Eve and followed her closely through the tall, jungle grass while they tried to find Adamu.

In the science lab of Eridu, two of the science officers were huddled over the amber glow of a domed crystalline monitor as one of them reached over and touched a yellow crystal panel located on the computer's console.

"Lord Enki," he said as he continued to monitor his viewing

screen.

"Acknowledged," Enki's voice said, as it came through the intercom speaker.

"My lord…there seems to be some kind of an issue with the male human. Our surveillance cameras have just picked up this transmission."

From his office in Eridu, Enki could see Adamu, stumbling about through the jungle franticly. He was absolutely terrified as he looked around, scared and nervous. Enki adjusted the image, and it pulled back to a yellow holographic display of the area's topography. The image pulled in again to show an infrared image of Eve. She was running after Adamu. Eve seemed to be accompanied by what looked like a large snake that moved on the ground alongside her. Enki's eyes widened in disbelief.

"*Lilith!*" he said to himself angrily.

Enki wheeled around in his chair. *How could she be inside the estate's perimeter?* With a scowl on his face, he abruptly pushed one of the orange crystal panels on his desks console.

"Lucifer! Report to my quarters. Immediately!"

Lucifer arrived at Enki's office very soon after, meeting him in the doorway. Enki gave him a sharp, angry look as he motioned for him to accompany him.

"Come with me," he said.

Above the mist covered foliage of the small streams that ran through bottom of the palace's smooth metallic corridors, Lucifer followed Enki along the brightly lit glass causeway to the nearest exit.

Once outside the Palace of Eridu, they got on personal gyro-electric transport cycles, where they quickly and silently made their way into the jungle interior of Edin. The rainforest was lit only by the glow of a full moon, but the roads they traveled were illuminated by streetlights that came on as their vehicles approached them.

They eventually reach a small jungle pathway, where they get off their bikes and park them. Unsheathing his sword, Lucifer walks with Lord Enki along the well-manicured, jungle path, lit only by the light of the full moon and they soon hear the sound of Adamu and Eve down the trail. Eve was softly consoling Adamu, who was hunched down, shaking and mumbling to himself incoherently.

When Lilith heard Enki's approach in the distance, she reared up her snake body in a defensive stance. She then morphed back into her human form and stood facing the approaching Anunaki lords with defiance in her eyes. Abruptly, the lights along the trail came on. Startled, Adamu and Eve looked up, frightened and bewildered.

"Lilith!" Enki yelled angrily. "What are you doing here?"

Lilith held her ground, clenching her hands into fists. She looked at him as he approached, not knowing exactly how to feel. He had hurt her deeply, but deep down inside, she still had strong feelings for him.

"If you must know...I had *originally* returned to your gardens to reclaim the legacy of our love!" she told him. "But upon my return, I find that I have become a *stranger* to you, and am unwelcome here. You had me shut out...and posted a guard!" She angrily wiped away the tears that began to well in her eyes.

"Even your brother could see me for who I am. *He* accepted me and gave me gifts of power! He is in truth, more of a man than you will *ever* be!"

Enki was quite surprised by this as he looked over at Lucifer, who stood silent.

"Is this true?" Enki asked him. "Have you fallen in love with my creation? This...human female?"

Lucifer stared at the ground. After a moment, he looked up and addressed his cousin eye to eye.

"Yes, it's true," he said.

Enki frowned and he puffed up his shoulders.

"But, my lord," Lucifer added, "you made her out to be some kind of hideous beast. I feel you were somewhat...deceptive."

Upon hearing Lucifer's response, Enki completely lost his patience and his temper. He rose his arms up and blasted Lucifer with an unseen kinetic force from out of his hands.

Lucifer was literally thrown twenty feet through the air by the force... with the sword he carried flying from his grasp. He landed with a thud, as the ancient ceremonial sword smashed on to the ground, breaking into many pieces. Lilith was shocked to see what Enki had done and she ran over to her fallen lover, kneeling down to see if he had been harmed.

Enki was furious. "How dare you question my motives, Captain!" He walked over to them and grabbed Lilith by the arm. "What have you *done*?" he demanded. He looked over at Adamu and Eve and walked over to them. Grabbing their faces with his large reptilian hands, he held them as he looked into their eyes.

"Psychotropic's...!" he growled. "You have given my creations psychotropic plants from the section of the garden that is specifically forbidden to them!" He released the humans and walked back over to where Lilith was standing and got right in her face. "You *have*, haven't you? What did you give them?"

Lilith kept her composure, not moving an inch... She would not be intimidated by him. She looked him squarely in the face.

"Amanita Muscaria."

Enki's eyes widened and his nostril slits flared. He looked over to Adamu and Eve and then back at Lilith.

"How *dare* you tamper with my creations!" He pointed over to a small pile of moss that Lilith had hidden under a bush with some plant cuttings in it. "The removal of clones from my garden is one thing... but tampering with the new workforce I am developing? *That* is a completely different offense!"

Enki swung his arms back in unison and then brought them around in front of him, his hands stopping just short of touching. In the space between them, a soft orange glow began to emanate.

"I am not one to be trifled with!" he shouted.

Looking down at his hands, Enki focused intensely on the

orange glow … and it became larger and brighter.

"Know that all I have created here," he said, "—I can just as easily *destroy!*"

Rearing back on his leg and tail, he lifts his other leg and slams his foot down. At the same time, he takes the ten-foot ball of orange energy he had created between his hands and forces it down into the ground in front of him.

A massive shockwave of wind and flames emanates from just outside an unseen, domed circular force field that closely surrounds and protects the group. The enormous blast quickly engulfs the land within Edin's interior in a huge wall of flames that lights up the night for miles in all directions. The veracious wall of flames instantly destroys all signs of life and vegetation. The Palace of Eridu is severely shaken by the blast, as landing beacons and palace spires are broken away by the intensity of the wind and flames.

As the tremors subside and the dust settles, the large main structure of the Palace of Eridu remained intact for the most part. The surrounding rainforest jungle however, had been burned to the ground and charred to a blackened crisp. The group find themselves standing within a circular patch of undamaged foliage, some twenty-five feet across, as they look around in wide eyed disbelief. The full moon illuminates the few small trees and bushes within the sphere that remained intact, as embers softly drift from the edges, singed where the dome that had enclosed and protected them had once been.

Under the light of the moon, Enki scrutinized the surrounding devastation with a smug satisfaction. "Bear witness to the repercussion of your actions!" he told them. Whipping around, he looked down at Lucifer, who was still lying on the ground.

"You … my once most trusted of brothers. You were to keep this one *out!*" He scowled as he looked at Lilith. "And yet, you turned a blind eye to my instructions. Because of this"—he pointed in the direction of Eridu—"you will never again see the inside of the Palaces of Edin! You are to be exiled and hereby stripped of your ranking and authority, never again welcome in Edin, or anywhere else within the regiment of the Anunaki."

"Because of your compassion toward this human female," Enki continued, "you will be accursed. May this love ultimately drain you of your *very* life force."

He looked at Lilith. "And you! Not only have you tampered with my creation…you have spurned my love and chosen another! You too shall be accursed. Accursed to love no one—no matter how hard you may try.

"You have tasted the science of our immortality…so you shall never die. But struggle and endure for evermore—you will."

In his mind's eye, Enki watches a vision of the predicted events of prophecy unfold within his head.

"In your many years, your womb shall bear children in great number," he explained.

Enki sees Lilith lying in a bed as she gives birth to a light-skinned baby with pointed ears. The vision shifts…it is early evening and Lilith is in a garden pavilion. Standing before her, in a large courtyard, is a group of fair-skinned, longhaired elfin-looking people of all ages. They are her children. They seem to not notice her standing there, as, in unison they all slowly turn away from her.

"But, your children will not love you—or even know you," he explained.

Enki's mental vision shifts again. It is night and the moon hangs full and heavy. Lilith is standing on an ocean bluff that overlooks the sea. She is alone.

"You will spend your life awake at night; the sun, the very element your new lover Lucifer has so ritualistically come to represent, will blind you during the day and burn your skin."

He turned and looked at her, "You may be considered an equal among my Elohim brothers, but a creature of the night you shall become!"

Enki now turned to Adamu and Eve, who were frightened and

huddled together. He walked over to confront them. The air was tense as he stood over the terrified humans, just looking at them, surmising their fate.

"I have tried to make your life comfortable here," he said, "but you have shunned my graces. You have eaten from the forbidden section of my gardens when you were told quite specifically not to." He paused. "Adamu—just as you had rejected the first mate that I made for you, I shall remove you from *my* graces as well," he told him. "You will be cursed to toil until your dying days. As you have mated with the beasts of the field, you shall be as one with them in your lust. And as I let you name the world around you... you will be doomed to confuse your words throughout your existence," he assured him. "You have also raised your hand in dominance to your woman... so, she shall dominate *you* throughout your days. Strong as you may be."

He looked at Eve, and this time his voice was softer. "Eve... the beauty of your innocence now... escapes me. You have partaken of a substance—a substance that I had *specifically* forbidden to you," he said angrily.

"You shall be removed from my graces as well!"

Eve is suddenly confronted by an emotion she has never felt as a great sadness overwhelms her, and her eyes begin to well with tears.

"Where I would have just as easily let you and your mate stay here indefinitely to live out your days in these gardens tending to the dinner tables of Edin's palaces... I would have been content to have simply bred your children to create my workforce." His voice grew stern. "You and Adamu will now be sent down to a breeding facility in the Abzu, where the two of you will begin creating my new workforce immediately. And you too shall be accursed, my dear Eve. You shall toil until the end of your days as well. Your egg cycle will be multiplied, so that your womb will bear many offspring throughout your lifetime," he told her, "Just as you have lusted for the forbidden plants in my garden, you will lust for the seed of man until the end of your days."

As Enki ponders Eve's fate, in his mind he sees a vision of a pregnant Eve as she lay in a bed. Wide-eyed and covered in sweat...she is screaming as she endures a painful child delivery.

He turned and looked at her sharply. "As traumatic as the events that have transpired here today, so shall be the trauma you will experience while giving birth to your many children! May it *forever* be a painful reminder of what has happened here today."

He now stood back and addressed the humans with a rather nonchalant indifference. "The knowledge of what is truly good and evil now rests within you both." He looked at them with narrowed eyes. "But in time—that knowledge will be misplaced—and you will forget."

Everyone looked blankly at Enki as he paused for a moment and lowered his head. He stared at the ground as he began to fully realize the depth of the repercussions of his own actions.

"As for my fate," he announced, "I too, shall be accursed for what has happened here today."

"For ultimately, it was *I* who allowed all of this to come to pass," Enki said. He looked at his captain of the guard. "In my haste, I may not have been fully forthcoming. Lucifer...I should have warned you of Lilith's grace and beauty, for I too had opened my heart to her and became easily taken by her captivating ways." He looked at Lilith. "As so, I shall forever keep the gates of my heart guarded. Although I will surely take a mate in the future—I will never *love* again." He turned from the group as he stared off into the distance.

Lilith and Lucifer exchanged glances and they whispered softly to each other. "What makes him so sure of these fates?" Lilith said to him under her breath. "Just who does he think he is?"

Lucifer got up off the ground and Lilith stood partially hidden behind him as he confronted his cousin.

"Lord Enki...with all your power," he shouted, "Who are *you* to curse us with these fates? You're one of *us*!"

"It is not *I* who has cursed you," Enki responded. "These fates are the result of your own actions! Laws to which we are *all* bound."

Enki turned to face them. "Soon, we will gather before the assembly of the Great Council." He gestured toward the darkened fields of devastation that surrounded them.

"The Elohim will want to know what has transpired here today. Then and there will the Great Council bear witness to the righteousness of these claims. They will be the ones to determine whether or not these events shall truly come to pass."

Chapter Twenty-five

The lights of the approaching aircraft could be seen in the distance and within moments, three shuttlecraft descend upon the small circular patch with a great blast of wind as they touch down. Their doors opened and a squad of armed reptilian guards quickly exit the crafts to surround the group and hold their drawn weapons on them.

Adamu and Eve were huddled together in fear, and tears came to Lilith's eyes, as Lucifer hung his head in sorrow. Ninutra was in charge of the assault team and stepped forward to address Enki.

"Lord Enki!" he said sternly. "Lord Enlil *demands* your immediate council. You and your group are to come with me at once."

The armed guards escort them all into the shuttlecrafts: Enki in one, Lilith and Lucifer in one, and Adamu and Eve in the other. The three transports then lift off and head toward the charred palace of Eridu off in the distance.

Escorted by armed guards down Eridu's brightly lit silver corridors, Enki and his group walk along long, raised-glass causeways that passed over lush green plants, small streams and soft swirling ground mists. They were being taken to the Grand Council Hall. Eventually they come to a large, elaborate door, tapered at its archways. Slowly, the massive doors of the Great Hall open and the group are escorted in.

The vaulted ceiling of the large dark circular hall was huge, dwarfing the group as they entered the room. The center of the Great Hall was dark, but up above, from the center of the high ceiling, hung an enormous quartz crystal that gave a glow that filled the rest of the hall with soft light. They were taken to the dimly lit edge of the large hall, where a small waiting area sat tucked below the bleachers that lined the walls. Seated on benches, they waited —everyone relatively calm except for Adamu and Eve, who, uncertain of their fate, were quite frightened. They held each other closely as they anticipated what was to come.

After some time had passed, dark, hooded figures slowly began to emerge from the numerous darkened doorways among the many benches that lined the walls of the Council Hall. One by one, the hooded council members slowly began to fill the chamber's many rows of dimly lit bleachers.

Numbering fifty, the Great Council had finally gathered. In the holding area, a light came on abruptly, illuminating Enki's group.

Out of the darkness, a single voice spoke. It was Enlil.

"Lord Enki…firstborn son of Anu."

Enki rose from his seat. He remained poised and confident as his tail flicked subtly with an attentive expectation of the events that were about to take place.

Another light came on abruptly, lighting up the enormous, raised hexagon quartz crystal dais located in the center of the large room. Thirty feet across, it was rooted into the center of the Great Hall, as a brilliant white light emanated from the base at its core, illuminating the massive quartz crystal from within. Seven High Council members sat in dark, elaborately spiked chairs on top of the great crystals' flattened hexagonal surface at each of the six points, with the seat at the center significantly raised. The hoods of their heavy cloaks hid their darkened, reptilian faces.

Revealing his shadowed face, the High Council member in the dais' center chair slowly pulled back his hood: it was Lord Enlil.

The rest of the High Council followed suit, revealing the various horned craniums of lords—Astarte, Tammuz, Nannar, Ninutra, Lady Ninlil, and Lady Ama-arhus. Ninmah and members of Enki's immediate family were not allowed to be part of the council because they were thought to be too close to the accused and what had happened.

"The Great Council requires an explanation of the events that have transpired here today," Enlil announced. A low murmur arose from the council members who filled the Hall.

With a hint of arrogance to his stance, Enki remained calm as he looked around the darkened room with a narrow-eyed scrutiny.

Enlil stood abruptly and pointed his finger accusingly at Enki.

"Lord Enki...step forward. Tell us *why* our Earth base estate of Edin has been reduced to a charred wasteland!"

Enki stepped up to the podium. He explained to the council the whole story of what had happened within the gardens and of the human's participation in a substance that could very well jeopardize the entire earth operation. He explained his fury with Lilith for tampering with the human's consciousness and his decision to set an example. In conclusion, he then explained his claims regarding the repercussions of what had happened.

After he gave his account of all that had happened, Lucifer and Lilith calmly explained their sides of the story. After all three were finished, there was a great uproar in the hall among the Assembly. As the murmurs died down, a single reptilian voice spoke out.

"Lord Enki should be severely reprimanded for what has happened here today," the voice said. "Look at what he has done to the complex of Eridu and our gardens within the Edin...they have been utterly destroyed! Enki has transformed our Earth base into a charred and devastated *wasteland!*"

The room exploded with an uproar of disapproval. A voice sounded out above the rest, this one strong and elderly. It spoke out, "It is Lilith who must pay for her crimes! It was she who enticed the human female to partake in the forbidden psychotropic plant in the first place."

The room exploded in an uproar again; eventually, another voice spoke, deep and resonant, "Lucifer is to blame for this catastrophe! His duties as head of the compound's security are quite clear! He has become seduced by the Lilith creature. Upon giving away his gifts of power, Lucifer has compromised his duties as head of Anunaki security!"

The Great Hall went into a heated frenzy once again as the Elohim argued among themselves. After a moment, another cold and calculating reptilian voice spoke out above the rest, "It is the *humans* that are to blame for all of this! They are potentially too dangerous to be trusted!"

A loud, ominous uproar of approval rang throughout the Hall.

"The unpredictable powers of these advanced mammals could *never* be insured against…no matter how much field dampening is imposed!" he proclaimed. Another roar of approval filled the Great Hall. "If a simple plant can undo so much of the dampening that we have taken extensive measures to establish, then this new work-force must be completely redesigned!" He then shouted, "*Death* to the humans!"

The Great Assembly Hall lit up with rhythmic shouts of approval and the stomping of feet.

WHOOMPHH…WHOOMPHH…WHOOMPHH…

When the noise finally died down, the seven High Council members rose from their seats. They left the seating area on top of the giant crystal dais and slowly exited the Great Council Chamber through a recessed, darkened doorway to their private council chambers to discuss their verdict.

After a short recess, the High Council reemerged from the shadows and took their places on the raised crystal dais. Standing, they looked down on the accused who awaited their decisions. Lord Enlil stood central among them and he stepped forward. Taking a deep breath, he folded his arms as he looked down at

Enki and the rest of his group.

"The High Council has convened...and we are now ready to proclaim your fates," he said. He pointed at Enki, Lilith and Lucifer. "The three of you will have a chance to make your final statements before a Course of Manifestation is proclaimed." He then turned and pointed at Adamu and Eve. "As for the two humans...they are not recognized by this court." He continued, "Their fates shall be decreed now." He paused and said in a low, ominous voice, "Death..."

Not understanding what was happening; Adamu and Eve hear the rhythmic chanting and stomping starting up again.

WHOOMPHH...WHOOMPHH...WHOOMPHH...

Suddenly, black hoods are placed over their heads, and for them, everything goes dark.

✦ ✦ ✦

When the black hoods are finally removed, Adamu and Eve find themselves kneeling on charred, blackened ground standing next to each other. Two large reptilian guards remove their hand restraints, and then hurry off toward their transport craft and get inside. The ship then quickly flies away.

Adamu and Eve get up and look around. They now find themselves standing alone in the center of the vast, blackened wasteland of Edin.

Back in the Great Council Hall, the whole Grand Council observe the couple's plight through the holographic imagery inside of the large quartz crystal that hangs from the center of the high ceiling.

They all watch, as from out of nowhere, a dark ominous cloud begins to gather on the distant horizon. Holding each other closely, Adamu and Eve watch the dark mass in horror. The massive storm cloud quickly gathers into a violent cyclone of wind, water, lightning and charred debris, picking up in a cyclonic fury.

The dark, electrified mass moves quickly as it approaches the defenseless couple from across the blackened plains. Pelted by water and debris, Adamu scans his surroundings desperately, but finds nowhere to shelter them and nothing to shield them from the harsh elements of the intense storm. Quickly he positions Eve under his body to protect her from the ravages of the dark wall of fury that was almost upon them.

As soon as Enlil saw Adamu's protective behavior toward his mate, he reached out his clawed finger and touched a yellow crystal panel that caused the artificial cyclone to pull back and dissipate. In the stands, Ninmah was among the council members who were watching the sentencing unfold. She smiled whimsically to herself. She had had a feeling that in time, her brother would become intrigued by the humans' unique behavior traits.

The dark cloud dissipated almost as quickly as it appeared. In the early morning light, nothing but a hazy mist remained. Eve tried to help Adamu stand, as she looked at the sky in frightened bewilderment. Then, deep from the within the mist, a soft rustle could be heard. The sound got louder and louder as a definite rhythm became audible; it was the sound of animals running toward them.

Suddenly, a pack of ravenous wolves burst from the surrounding mist . . . and they were hungry. Their teeth gnashed ferociously and drool flung from their snarling jaws as they descended quickly upon the two unsuspecting humans with full force. Frightened, but without hesitation, Eve put her body between the attacking wolves and the disoriented, defenseless Adamu. The pack of wolves bore down quickly upon the couple, then hurled themselves at the two humans with ferocity, teeth gnashing.

A great commotion in the Council Chamber among the Elohim began again when Enlil pressed another crystalline panel.

From out of nowhere, a domed, transparent, electronic force field manifests around the two defenseless humans, closely surrounding and protecting them. The wolves hit the invisible force field abruptly and let out loud, injured cries as they painfully bounce off the protective dome, yelping from their injuries.

Confused, Adamu and Eve huddle together in terror, as the pack of angry wolves snap at them ferociously just outside the invisible force field's perimeter.

Chapter Twenty-six

Before the Assembly, Enlil gestured toward the hologram within the giant crystal that displayed the captured video surveillance account of Adamu and Eve in the charred wilderness as they faced first the storm and then the wolves. He stood and addressed the council members, who were still quite restless.

"I am intrigued by these humans…they seem to exhibit a highly unique behavioral trait in that they are willing to sacrifice themselves to preserve their kindred." There was a murmur of concurrence with the Great Hall. "The increased sense of devotion that these creatures carry for one another could potentially be a very valuable asset to us within the dangerous work environments of the Abzu."

He touched the control panel. The hologram within the viewing crystal now showed a time stamped image of five Lulu workers mining within a large earthen cavern next to an open fissure that went deep into the earth. One of the Lulu suddenly lost his foot hold on a ledge next to the dark, cavernous hole. As he slipped, he managed to catch himself on the edge of the cliff. Looking up in desperation, he reached out helplessly to a nearby coworker for assistance.

The other Lulu worker paused in his activities and casually looked over at his fallen brethren with large, dark empty eyes. The creature did nothing to react to its coworker's dilemma and slowly turned its head back to continue its work. The Lulu on the ledge grasped desperately at the ground as it lost its hold and fell into the dark abyss.

"This preservation quality in the humans would prove to be to our advantage in hazardous mining environments," Enlil said. "Fewer replacement workers would ultimately endorse higher productivity levels."

Many of the council members agreed with him as they nodded among themselves in concurrence. "With the approval of the High Council," he continued, "we *will* allow the human experiment and proceed with their breeding."

The council members murmured and nodded among themselves again. Ninmah was pleased and somewhat relieved that she would not be called upon again for the tedious task of redesigning another work force for their mission here on Earth.

Enlil spoke into the computer console, "Retrieve the humans," he said. "Have them sent to the breeding stables in the Eastern Abzu outpost of Nod." The filtered voice of one of his lieutenants responded to the request. "Yes, my lord."

Having now addressed the issue of the humans, Enlil turned his attention to Enki, Lilith and Lucifer.

"The council is ready to hear your final statements," Enlil said, coldly. "Step forward, Lucifer."

Lucifer stepped forward and stood upon the raised dais to address the High Council. The golden cream scales of his lean, muscular body and his fine, golden horns shimmered in the stark light of the brightly lit platform. He looked up at his fellow Anunaki.

"Great Council... I have only done what was asked of me by Lord Enki. I was told to beware of a hideous beast...with hate in its heart. If I have erred in my actions, it was in the shadow of Lord Enki's unwillingness to be forthcoming." There were murmurs among the Elohim. "The creature Lilith is of *his* design. He knows what she is." He shot a look over to Enki. "Lilith is an absolutely amazing creature who has become so *very* much...an equal among ourselves!"

He looked over to see Lilith smiling at him.

"Lilith has become what she is by her own design," he continued. "As such...I *do* love her." He puffed up proudly. "I am content in her...and I could never despise her wishes." He looked around at all of the hooded council members with a serene look of confidence in his eyes and on his face, then bowed his head. "In this...I proclaim my defense, my lords." On that, Lucifer turned and left the platform. He looked at Lilith reassuringly as she walked past him to take her place on the stand. She smiled back at him with a deep adoration.

Lilith stood on the defense platform and addressed the Council Hall. "My lords of the Assembly," she turned to address the High Council directly. "At first...I had returned to Edin to reclaim the legacy of my lover and creator, Lord Enki." She looked over at Enki with indifference, as he sat complacently in a side area. Her eyes narrowed and her mild look quickly turned to one of subtle anger and scorn.

"Upon my return," she continued, "I found that Lord Enki... had personally set up an armed guard to keep me out, as if I were an unwanted stranger!" Her eyes widened in disbelief as she looked up at the room of council members. "And yet his closest of brothers could see me for who I truly am." She looked over at Lucifer. "He gave me gifts of love and power. In this, I would never renounce him, nor relinquish the love that I carry for him." She paused as she looked around the room. "As for my behavior in the gardens," she added, "I had become accustomed to certain fruits at my table... fruits that were denied to me by Lord Enki!" She shot him a sharp look, but he didn't respond and just looked at her blankly.

"My lords...I long to taste the sweet nectar of strawberries, honeydew and papaya, as well as the many other succulent fruits that have been brought here from your home world and other-world travels. Although I have tried on countless occasions, the genetic makeup within most of these plant strains are extremely complex and very difficult to reproduce. My many attempts had always ended in failure," she explained.

"And as for the humans..." Lilith paused for a moment. "Well, they are intriguing. One cannot help but *wonder* at their potential. I admit my curiosity may have been a bit...unreserved, but I ask you my lords: is this *not* a mission of exploration?"

Upon her closing statements, she turned to the High Council, bowed down on one knee to show her respect and then rose to leave the stand. As she returned to the defendants' holding area, she looked over at Lucifer, who gently closed his eyes as he nodded toward her approvingly. He was proud of her.

It was now Lord Enki's turn and he got up to take the stand. The hall lit up again with an unruly commotion. He stood on the raised dais ready to address his brethren and the noise slowly subsided.

"Members of the Grand Assembly...you have witnessed my claims of prophecy." He looked about the room and declared, "Their repercussions are *our* curses to bear!" He then turned to the High Council. "I make no claims of remorse for my part in what has happened here." Looking around at the room full of hooded council members, he folded his arms confidently and spoke with authority.

"I am...what I am!" he declared.

The Great Hall filled with the murmurs of the Anunaki elite.

Enlil glanced at the members of his council, then stood up and pointed at Enki. "Lord Enki, firstborn son of the Lord King Anu... The High Council is in concurrence with the wisdom in your claims of prophecy." He raised his arms and looked skyward. "We will allow your predictions to come to manifestation." Lowering his arms, he then gestured toward the other two. "Lucifer and Lilith will not be welcome in Edin...they are to be banished." He then pointed at Enki sternly. "You, Lord Enki, will return to your duties in the mines of the Abzu...*after* you have replanted and completely repaired the estate grounds of Edin."

The Great Hall was silent as Enki looked about the room with an arrogance he did very little to conceal. He left the lit platform content and quickly removed himself from the Great Hall through a darkened, recessed doorway at its edge. Lilith and Lucifer got up from where they were separately seated and left the defenses' holding area and met on the dimly lit central causeway in a passionate embrace. Escorted by two guards, they left arm in arm through the large main doorway of the Great Hall.

Chapter Twenty-seven

At Edin's southern gate, amidst a blackened wasteland, the thin force field of orange fire was active as it curves off in both directions for as far as the eye can see. Accompanied by their two large reptilian guards, Lucifer and Lilith sift through the charred debris of Lucifer's old outpost.

Straying a moment from where Lucifer was rummaging through the soot, Lilith wanders off to inspect a nearby area.

As she was walking, something on the ground glimmers in the dark ashes. Kneeling down, she blows away the surface ashes and discovers the remnants of the cape that Lucifer had given her, the diamond galaxy swirl pattern of her cloak being still partially intact on the ground where she had hidden it.

She scoops up the pile of glimmering stones and put them into a small pouch that she carries on her belt. Standing up, she turns and hurries back to Lucifer to show him what she has discovered.

She put her hand on his arm, and as she showed him the contents of her pouch, and the large lizard man beamed proudly in appreciation of her find. He showed her the few charred items of his that he was able to salvage: an ancient ceremonial sword and a small sun emblem. Lilith smiled as she put her arm around his waist, knowing how important the ceremonial items were to him. They then turned from the ruins and made their way toward the estate's large reticulated gateway, with their guards following at a respectful distance.

The massive, dark metallic gateway looms before them as they approach it, and after they pass through, the large reticulated doorway closes silently behind them. In the aftermath of all that had happened, they leave Edin, banished.

As the two walked away from the massive gate that penetrated the force field of fire surrounding Edin's estate, Lilith looked up at Lucifer, concerned for their future.

"My love, what is to become of us now?"

He stopped for a moment, then turned to her and looked deeply into her eyes. She held his hand and they sat down on the ground together. Lucifer curled his thick, golden beige tail gently around the two of them as he looked at Lilith with a deep adoration and took a moment to contemplate her question.

"No one can be absolutely certain, my love. But I *can* tell you this... The lords of the High Council will no doubt want to take the human design to their labs and raise up human creations of their own. Adamu and Eve have now been sent to the breeding facility of Nod, where they will be well taken care of. But, in time ...you can be *assured* that the Anunaki will teach the humans to fear and despise us."

Lilith closed her eyes and nodded, silently acknowledging the wisdom of his words.

"Lord Enki will remain among the Elohim and continue his duties as a High Anunaki official." Lucifer took a deep breath. "But, he will most likely become reclusive within his own *personal* exile."

The two were taken by a deep sadness as they reflected. Shaking it off, Lucifer stood up and reached out for Lilith's hand. She stood up and he looked into her eyes.

"As for you and me...I will go with you to your garden estate of D'hainu and there we will raise a family of our own."

Lilith looked up at him and smiled.

"In time, you will bear for me three fine sons, and we will name them...Kessep, Shotheq, and Nesher." He pulled her close and held her in a passionate embrace. "You will also bear three fine daughters, whom we will name—Mem, Oreb, and Laylah." Lilith smiled as she looked up at him, content in his predictions for their future.

Leaving Edin, Lilith and Lucifer held each other tightly as they walked arm in arm toward the gray, cloud-filled horizon, far off in the distance.

Lightning Source UK Ltd.
Milton Keynes UK
UKHW040716010722
405240UK00001B/40